# Samuel'

Brenda W. Craddock

First published in Great Britain as a softback original in 2018



All characters and events in this book, other than those clearly in the public domain, are fictitious and any resemblance to real persons, living or dead, is purely coincidental.



Typeset in Dante MT Std

Editing, typesetting and publishing by UK Book Publishing

UK Book Publishing is a trading name of Consilience Media

www.ukbookpublishing.com

ISBN: 978-1-912183-41-8

# Chapter 1

Millie was feeling her age. She worked hard as a cleaner at 'The Strawberry' pub and also at Snow Street School, which was close to where she lived. She was 70 years old and had always been told she looked young for her age, but it was no longer true. The shock of Samuel's disappearance, and dealing with Arthur's illness, had affected her looks she was sure. Even now she had bad dreams about certain parts of her life and she could not remember the last time she had felt really happy. That day, 20 years ago, when their son had left home and never returned, had consequences which changed their lives for ever. She was grateful, however, that she still had one daughter, a son-in-law and a granddaughter, who brought some light into her life and she must be thankful for that. They had helped her to survive, while she clung onto the hope that one day she would be reunited with her beloved son Samuel.

These reflections were going through her mind as she walked home that morning from 'The Strawberry'. It had been a tough morning because the pub was very dirty from the night before. There had been a party and it looked as if beer had been thrown everywhere. The walls were splashed and the floor sticky and it had badly needed scrubbing. Kneeling down made her knees sore and her back ache and standing up from a kneeling position was getting more and more difficult. There was even glass on the floor and on some of the tables and Millie had to pick her way carefully across the floor to avoid stepping on the glass.

It would be so good not to have to get up so early for work. She had been up since half past four this morning because she had to be at work for half past five and she liked to be on time. She had to keep on working because she needed the money. There was no-one now bringing in an extra wage and her daughter Esther, who lived a few streets away, needed the money she earned for her own family. If only Arthur had lived and Samuel had not gone away things would have been very different, but she was not so badly off as some families she knew. She also knew that lives were not built on 'if only'. It was a futile exercise following that line of thought. She would be glad when she was safely back to her beloved small house in Douglas Terrace.

She lived alone but she did not mind that. She liked having her own space but she also liked having friends and her house was always open to them. She was known for her warm hospitality. There was always a cup of tea and a scone for anyone who called. Even though she said it herself, she made delicious scones.

Esther had stayed at home with her for quite a long time after Arthur died and after Samuel had gone away and she was very grateful for that, but she had always wanted her daughter to marry one day and she had, in 1919, just after the First World War had ended. Her husband was a young man she had met while working in an office in Gallowgate, and they had bought a small house in Stanhope Street, which was conveniently near Douglas Terrace where Millie lived. Their daughter Sarah had been born after five years of marriage in 1924 and she had brought such joy. Millie had been thrilled to be involved with babies again and it was very good that she now had plenty to do helping Esther with the baby. She loved babies and children and loved the company of her daughter, son-in-law and granddaughter, as they helped to fill the dark hole in Millie's world, which had once also included her husband, Arthur, daughter Rachel and son Samuel.

Having a baby in her arms again, at the age of 65, had been a great comfort to her and she could at last see a future without those three people who had been so precious to her.

Her friends had been delighted to see Millie so happy, after the gruelling time she had had nursing her husband. She was such a kind lady, who would help anyone and they were delighted that she now had a granddaughter upon whom she could lavish attention. She would be the perfect grandma.

The man for whom Millie worked and who owned 'The Strawberry' was very good to her. The pub had stood for many years in the area of Gallowgate, in the west end of the city of Newcastle. There was a lot of uncultivated land around it now, but early in the 19th century, the land had been cultivated into strawberry fields which were looked after by the nuns of St. Bartholomew's, whose nunnery was not far away in Newgate Street. The nunnery survived until 1850 by selling strawberry wine, despite being threatened by the Bishop of Durham with excommunication.

Over time the strawberries withered and the land was neglected until it looked like waste land, but 'The Strawberry' had survived the changes, which had taken place in this area and its owner, Mr Jack Riddell, for whom she worked had told her the story of it. A man called John Brunton owned quite a large house on the land at Gallowgate at the end of the 18th century and stated that his house had to remain standing, when other houses on that land were demolished and he also said that the lower part of it had to be used as a beer house. His orders were carried out, although by the middle of the 19th century only the lower part of the house was retained and the pub was called 'The Strawberry' because of the strawberry fields that had surrounded it in former times. The nearby streets bore the names 'Strawberry Place' and 'Strawberry Lane'.

Millie quite enjoyed the walk home from the pub every day. She had grown to be fond of that area, which she had known from a very young age. The football field had not been there when she was a young child but it was there now and the grounds of Newcastle United were almost opposite the pub where she worked.

Newcastle United football team had been formed in 1892 and Arthur, her husband, was a keen supporter, so she was very familiar with the football ground. They had watched the football ground being erected in 1892.

Millie had lived in the West end of Newcastle all her life. Her parents had once lived in Stowell Street and that was where she had been born and brought up. When she and Arthur married they had lived in a very small house off Westgate Road, but when their family were still young they had moved into a slightly bigger house in Douglas Street. The reason for their move was to do with the education of their children. There were no government-run schools, in the early part of the 19th century, and no law saying children had to go to go to school. There were some schools called Ragged Schools, which provided basic instruction, meals and clothing and many children benefited from them, but few working …ss children had any formal education and certainly there was no … education for anyone at this time.

…nged in 1870, when an Education Act was passed an… …et up a National System of Board Schools, funde… …rthurs Hill Board School, in the west end of the … …rmanent schools set up by Newcastle School … …cation Act. It opened in 1875 to accommodate … …ickly gained a good reputation. The school changed its nam… …ng after it opened, to be known as Snow Street School, and i… …d adjoining baths and washhouse, reflecting the lack of good …hing facilities in houses towards the end of the 19th century. It …s for this reason that wash houses and baths were being built al… …r Newcastle at that time and they were usually attached to other buildings. Millie often used the washhouse and public baths, which were attached to Snow Street School. They were very convenient for her family.

Similar facilities had been built in Gallowgate in 1857 but had had to be demolished in 1895 when Gallowgate was widened to accommodate trams and they were a great miss to everyone in the area. It was a bonus for Millie and her neighbours that they had the Snow Street baths and wash house close to them because it was quite a long walk to Gallowgate, from where they lived.

Arthur and Millie had always wanted a good education for their children and Snow Street School was the school which all Millie's children attended.

There were many streets of houses surrounding the school, which were built 'back to back' with a cobbled back lane running between the back yards. These lanes in the 19th century were a perfect place to play safely, and there was a tremendous community spirit in this area and others like it. All the children made friends and enjoyed going to school together. It was an experience entirely new for them and made such a difference to their lives. Without realising it they were accumulating knowledge and learning all sorts of skills which would help to build their future.

Arthur and Millie had shown great foresight in moving to an area where their children could receive the best education available at that time for working class families. It was very different for children whose parents were wealthy, but certainly their parents could not have been any more caring and loving than those from poorer backgrounds.

The parents who lived in the area around Snow Street, or Arthurs Hill, were a small group but had a genuine sense of community. Everyone helped one another, particularly when there was a crisis of any kind. This could mean anything from a child being born to the laying out of someone after death. No-one ever wanted to go to hospital or call out the doctor and they prided themselves on always being a caring, protective and supportive community. It was a good place to live and Millie and her beloved family thrived and loved living there.

That was why in 1929, at 70 years of age, she was still living there and had no intention of ever leaving.

# Chapter 2

Millie and Arthur had both been born during the reign of Queen Victoria and they admired her very much. She had married for love, and her 'Beloved Albert' and herself gave a whole new meaning to family life. Children in the Victorian Era were not encouraged to talk, especially if at a social event with their parents. Victoria and Albert had nine children, each of whom was loved dearly and they wanted to spend time with their children, and live as a family.

The Royal Couple were not afraid to show their affection for one another and for their children and they talked and listened to them and even played games with them. They introduced their family to books and one of their favourite pastimes was reading to their children. The happiness of the Royal Family was evident, and proof that spending time with children and allowing them to join in conversations, was very beneficial to their learning about the world around them.

It was a tremendous shock to Victoria when her beloved husband Albert died in 1861 at Windsor Castle but she still tried to spend more time with her children, and as more books became available towards the latter part of the 19th century she encouraged the older ones to read and use their imaginations. The Victorians loved reading all kinds of literature, which meant novels, books of self-improvement, newspapers, magazines, travel guides, popular histories and even comics. There were no cinemas or televisions and so reading became a popular use of leisure time and it gave much pleasure.

As greater educational opportunities became available there was a greater need for books. The most popular Victorian writer was Charles Dickens. He had written his first novel 'The Pickwick Papers' in 1837 and it was a great success. His second novel was 'Oliver Twist' and these novels were followed by many others, all of which greatly appealed to his readers because they were based on true facts of Victorian Society. Dickens was able to write with compassion and with humour about the social injustices of his time. There were some wonderful characters in his books including Mr Micawber, Bill Sykes, Nancy, Fagin, and Scrooge.

Three other writers were significant in the Victorian period and they were the Bronte sisters. Charlotte wrote 'Jane Eyre' in 1847, Emily 'Wuthering Heights' in the same year and the younger sister Anne, 'Tenant of Wildfell Hall' in 1848.

Quite a number of books were written especially for children during Victoria's reign. Favourites were 'Treasure Island' by Robert Louis Stevenson, the two Jungle Books by Rudyard Kipling and Black Beauty by Anna Sewell. The books which Millie loved best were the children's picture books, produced by Kate Greenaway, just when she was growing up. Another book which was published in 1865, when she was 6 years old, was Alice in Wonderland by Lewis Carroll. It was a wonderful fantasy story. Alice had so many adventures and when she was very small Millie's mother had to read it to her over and over again.

Millie always associated reading with pleasure because one of her best memories of her mother, was sitting on her knee while she read stories to her and snuggling up when her mother pulled her in closely. It was a lovely secure feeling and as she grew older, her mother was able to point out different words, which led to her being able to read before she went to school.

Millie's love of reading never wavered and her mother, who was an avid reader herself and had been unable to buy books in quantity, as they were quite expensive to buy, had been very relieved when in 1850 the Public Libraries Act was passed and towns were able to use rates to build free libraries for all. Millie's mother had made great use of the facility to borrow books and she had been told that in the late 1700s, early 1800s, when she was a young girl, Newcastle had become a centre of the printing trade and its production of children's books was greater than any town outside of London.

Millie had tried to give her own children that secure cosy feeling when she read books to them. She herself still loved reading and was a regular visitor to the Free Central Library, in New Bridge Street, which had opened in 1880. The idea to open a free library there had been passed by the council in 1854 but it was not until 1880 that the library in New Bridge Street was opened. When the children were small Millie often pushed the pram down Gallowgate, to cross the road at Percy Street onto Blackett Street, then walk a short distance to the bottom of Northumberland Street, cross it and walk a short way down New Bridge Street until she reached the Library. It was quite a long way from Douglas Terrace so she only ever took the children when they were still in a pram. If Arthur accompanied her, as their family grew, it was easier because he could carry a toddler on his shoulders. It was harder pushing a pram home, because it was slightly uphill all the way, but Millie did not mind the exercise too much. It helped to keep her fit.

She tried to get her children to read before they went to school. Samuel was the only one to achieve that but he was the most intelligent of their three children. That had been obvious in the first year of his life, but of course Samuel was a very special little boy.

# Chapter 3

Millie and Arthur had taken notice of the example set by Queen Victoria and Albert and were very loving and caring parents, spending as much time with their family as they could. Their house was not too far from the River Tyne where Arthur worked in the Elswick Engineering Factory built and owned by Lord William Armstrong, and he could walk there from his home in Douglas Terrace. Millie and Arthur were not rich but Arthur worked hard and she was careful with the money he earned. She did not go out to work after the children were born – very few people did at that time, because a mother's place was thought to be in the home, looking after their children. Millie fully agreed with that sentiment and she loved motherhood. Arthur, her husband, and their three children were everything to her and Millie was dearly loved by them.

She had inherited a sewing machine from her mother and she delighted in making clothes for her daughters. Sewing machines were too expensive when they were first invented during the Victorian era, and only the rich could afford to buy one but as they gained in popularity, they became cheaper and were much more widely used by middle and working class people. Millie had clever fingers and experimented with making clothes for herself and her children. They were much admired by other mothers and it was not long before they were asking if she could make clothes for their children or even for themselves. She accepted orders from them but was careful not to overdo it, because it was very time-consuming. The little extra money it made for her family was, however, very welcome. Arthur and Millie took pride in seeing that their children were well fed, well clothed and well loved.

The house they had moved to in Snow Street was like so many at that time. It had two rooms upstairs, two rooms downstairs, and an outside toilet. They had little furniture but had the essential big tin bath, which could be filled and put beside the fire for bath time. One day they hoped to have an inside toilet and bathroom and even an extra bedroom so that the children would not all have to sleep in the same room, but they would have to save for a long time to achieve that. Millie delighted in keeping her home clean but not always tidy, because that was difficult to achieve with three children. Their children did not have many toys because they were expensive, but Millie's father was very clever at making wooden toys, which the children loved, and these could be strewn across the floor at the end of the day, despite efforts to make the children do some tidying. They were a very happy little family and Millie could never have imagined it any other way, but change is a part of life and things were going to change for this family.

# Chapter 4

As Millie walked home that day in 1929 after the party clean up, she could not help remembering the days when, now that her children were grown up, she came home from work and Arthur was there to greet her before going off to his work. Arthur always had the kettle on 'for a brew' and always greeted her with a hug and kiss. A cup of tea was just what she wanted now after her busy morning but she would have to make it herself, which was not quite the same.

Arthur was always interested in what she had to say and he would have become angry when she'd told him about the state of the pub. He would also have noticed how tired she was and told her to have a little nap. He had been such a good husband and she had loved him dearly. He was such a kind man and in her eyes very wise. They always talked things over and made decisions together and she trusted him implicitly.

That dark day when the light of their life had gone, though, Arthur was inconsolable. He was a broken man and as time passed he became more and more depressed, saying life had no meaning for him and there was nothing at all to live for. He even said that he wished the gallows had still been there on the Town Moor because he would have hanged himself.

Millie asked herself time and time again how he could possibly be thinking like that. She was devastated too when Samuel had disappeared from their lives but she felt his reaction to losing their son was very extreme. She even found herself thinking that there must be something she did not know about, but she pushed such thoughts away. Arthur was certainly not a secretive man and she felt she could tell him anything and he always said he could also tell her anything and they had a very close relationship. This made it all the more upsetting to see the man he had become. She just could not communicate with him in his very depressed state but she was as patient and tolerant as she could be because she had to be strong for her daughter Esther who was constantly worrying and tearful about her father's illness. Then he began losing weight at an alarming rate and looked dreadful. Towards the end of his life he sat in the rocking chair all day, moaning to himself and rocking the chair backwards and forwards. He was so thin and a shadow of the man he had been and it was almost a relief when he died because now his tortured mind was at rest and Millie found comfort in that.

Millie never found out the real reason for her husband's unbearable state of mind. In the early stages of his depression and when he could think coherently Arthur had often wondered what her reaction would have been if she had known the reason for his lack of interest in anything at all, even life itself. He realised that he had been a very foolish man but he had got himself into the situation and could not extricate himself from it.

One thing the whole experience had taught him was that he loved Millie and his family above everything else, and he was profoundly sorry for what he had done. If she ever found out it would affect her deeply and he wanted to save her from that. The shock could have driven her away forever and he could not risk that.

He was, in fact, a murderer, but no-one must ever know. No-one that is, except Samuel, who did know, but would never betray his father. His father was absolutely sure about that. He understood why his son wanted to get away from him but he could not tell anyone. It was unbearable keeping the secret from Millie because they had once shared everything and he could hardly bear to hear her loud, heart breaking sobs every day for weeks after Samuel had gone.

Millie had asked herself the same questions over and over again. Why had he left and why had he left during the night, without telling them why he was going away? What had been so bad that he found it necessary to leave home? There had been no disagreements or arguments and no indication at all that he planning to leave home, although, looking back, he had seemed on edge for a while and was subdued. She had asked him if anything was the matter but he had said no and to stop fussing. She recalled that both he and Arthur had been badly affected by that accident at the Rowing Regatta but that had been months ago and she had thought he had recovered from that. It was very uncharacteristic of him not to be thoughtful of others and especially for herself, because he had always been a thoughtful son and they were very close. Even now, after twenty years of not seeing him, she missed him terribly. Why, oh why, had he left home? She never found the answer to her question.

# Chapter 5

Arthur had always told Millie that she was very pretty but she had convinced herself that because of all that had happened in her life, she had lost her looks. She had always had sharp features and hated her nose, which was far too long and pointed, and she had not looked after her skin for years. One of her friends told her that there were creams sold to help with her skin and promised to take her into the town to buy some face creams, but she felt her skin had gone beyond anything that face creams could do...

Millie was a good height at 5ft 6 ins and very slender, although her father always said she was skinny and that her clothes would look much nicer if she put on some weight. Certainly, she was no longer smart. In the 'old' days as she called them she had taken pride in her appearance but not now. Who cared about what she looked like? And so each day she just pulled on a skirt and a blouse, followed by her 'wraparound 'pinny', because she needed to wear it for work, and she usually put on a cardigan before leaving the house, all without even glancing in a mirror, because she was not one bit interested in how she looked. It was fortunate that her hair was curly and did not require much attention because she only ever gave it one brush through. It had once been raven black and her son Samuel had inherited her dark curly hair. Despite making a resolve in the very beginning, that she would not allow thoughts of Samuel to rule her life, she could not stop herself from thinking about him at some time in the day, every day. He had been so special.

Millie may have had a very low opinion of herself but unknown to her, someone was taking an interest in her and thought she was very attractive. It was her employer, Mr Jack Riddell. He remembered her from their school days. She had been a pupil at Snow Street School, in the year below him, but obviously Millie did not recognise him. He remembered her as being a very happy little girl, full of life and everyone's friend. He had thought he recognised her when she came for the interview to work in his pub and this was confirmed when she told him where she lived, and which school she had attended. She did not seem as happy or as full of life as he remembered her, but there was no mistaking her fine bone structure and lovely curly hair, which had once been as dark as coal but was now streaked with grey due to her advancing years. It was her lovely blue eyes he had remembered through the years, because they seemed to be exceptionally blue and her dark eyebrows were the perfect foil for them. A number of boys in his class had fancied her.

One day he might be able to talk to her about their old school but he would choose the time. He noticed that she did not smile very much and he rarely heard her laugh so perhaps she had had a hard life, and something very painful had happened to her, which had made her very unhappy.

He knew all about pain and suffering because the baby he and his wife had longed for, many years ago, had died not long after the birth, and his wife had caught an infection in childbirth, from which she never recovered. Childbirth carried a lot of risk at the end of the 19th century and the beginning of the 20th.

The double blow had left him a lonely man but he was glad of his livelihood as a pub owner and at least he had plenty of company every night to take his mind off his troubles. He was also kept very busy, because his pub was very popular in the neighbourhood.

When Millie had arrived for work the morning after the party, he had noticed how tired she seemed to be and he apologised profusely for all the extra work she was going to have to do. The party the night before had become quite riotous and he was angry that these party people had shown no respect for his property. He was particularly angry about the glass, because someone could have been badly injured and the police could have been involved. The pub had a good reputation and he wanted it to remain so.

He knew Millie's age, because she had been the year below him at school. That meant she was 70 now, not a young woman and so she would be tired after she finished work. The thought came to him that this was a good time to ask her out for a meal and then go to the theatre, to make it a special treat.It would make up in some way for all the work she was going to have to do. There was a theatre on Westgate Road which was near to where they both lived.

This Theatre and Opera House had been opened on the 18th September 1867.From first opening it was a success and became an important part of the Theatre scene in Newcastle. Until then the Theatre Royal was considered the best theatre in Newcastle, situated as it was in the centre of the city, on Grey Street, and that street was considered the most elegant street in Newcastle, if not the country. Its productions were considered the best but The Tyne Theatre Opera House quickly gained a very good reputation and also featured some excellent productions. It had superb acoustics as a result of its walls being lined with wood and was an excellent example of a Victorian Opera House.

The years leading up to the First World War were difficult financially and the theatre had to resort to showing moving pictures, which were not nearly as good as a live theatre production. After the war, in 1919, the theatre closed for restoration and modernisation and it reopened as 'The Stoll Picture Theatre' and was the first cinema to show 'Talking Movies' which were becoming very popular, but the theatre never really recovered its excellent reputation.

Jack was sure, however, that Millie would enjoy a 'Talking Movie' and decided that that was where he would take her.

He remembered his mother telling him that she and his father had spent some lovely evenings at that theatre, when it was live theatre. She used to dress up in her best clothes and make it a special occasion every time. She and her husband would sit hand in hand and he was at his most affectionate and romantic on these occasions. She cherished those memories.

Jack Riddell had intended to catch Millie when she finished her shift the morning of the big clean Up but he got involved with something else and by the time he remembered, he knew she would be on her way home. He must try to catch her tomorrow. He felt quite excited thinking about asking someone out on a date. He had never bothered with anyone else since Lizzie died but somehow it seemed a good idea to ask Millie out. He vowed to himself that he would do it soon.

# Chapter 6

On her way home from 'The Strawberry' Millie would be walking in the area of Gallowgate, which was a very old part of Newcastle in the west end of the city and it was very historic. In medieval times there had been simple houses and shops with yards and gardens but they were all taken down in the 13th century to make room for a town wall which was going to surround Newcastle as a defence from enemies.

When the wall was no longer needed after the civil war in 1644, when it was besieged by Scottish forces, who penetrated the walls, it was left to deteriorate, and parts of it were demolished. The land behind the wall at the St. Andrew's church in Gallowgate was left to waste and gallows were erected there, for the hanging of criminals. When the gallows were eventually removed in the middle of the 19th century the land was used by butchers before they slaughtered their cows and it was not a nice place to be because of the odours which inevitably pervaded the area. People avoided it if they could.

Fortunately, when Millie had to pass that way, it was clear of anything unhealthy. Arthur's mother had told Arthur and Millie early in their marriage that she had gone to see the last criminal to be hanged on the gallows at Gallowgate in 1844. The man who was hanged was called Mark Sherwood, and he had lived in Blandford Street. He had killed his wife and was taken, sitting on his own coffin, from gaol to the gallows, through the Gallow Gate to the land behind it.

Watching a person hang must surely be a gruesome experience, but a hanging always attracted crowds of people and there was plenty of jeering, shouting, mocking and scornful laughter and generally rowdy behaviour. Sometimes it got out of control as people pushed further and further forward to get a good view. It could be frightening but it did not deter the crowds, who looked at it as a form of entertainment, and came back time and time again.

Millie had commented to her mother-in-law that she thought the whole idea was barbaric and nothing would have made her go to a public hanging. It made her shiver to think how criminals must have felt as they approached the gallows and the end of their lives. It was such a cruel death and so humiliating, and she could not help wondering if any of the criminals ever repented of their crimes and if any of them ever asked to be forgiven for their crimes, before they faced death. She was very glad that the gallows had been taken down before she was born in 1859.

Nellie had nothing to say to that, except to say that crime was a feature of all Victorian towns and cities and the gallows were fully acceptable as a way of punishment at that time. Millie was still glad that she had never seen the gallows. It was bad enough hearing about them.

As an adult, however, Millie had read about crime and punishment in Victorian Society because she was a keen reader of Charles Dickens who was a great writer of the 19th century. He highlighted in his books many of the injustices, cruelties, crimes and punishments of Victorian society and sometimes his books made her cry, especially when she read about children who were very badly treated, through no fault of their own.

Millie's father once frightened Millie, when she was a young girl, by telling her gruesome tales of hangings and murderers in the North of England. She had found it difficult to sleep after those stories, and the next morning she asked her father if there was any protection for people who never committed crimes. 'Yes is the answer to your question, Millie. In 1829, a man called Sir Robert Peel set up a special metropolitan police force in London, who became known as 'Peelers' or 'Bobbies' after the man who set up the force and by 1856 almost all towns had a policeman who wore special uniforms and patrolled certain areas.'

'Thank goodness for that,' said Millie.

Millie and her siblings had been brought up strictly and knew the difference between right and wrong. They knew that they would be punished if they did anything wrong and they knew that their father kept a leather belt in a drawer, which he would use if necessary. Once her brother had been caught taking some washing off a lady's washing line in her back yard. He said it was just done for a dare and he didn't really want to do it. Oh dear, he had been terrified when his father opened the drawer that contained the leather belt, lifted it out and waved it in the air. Her mother started to cry and tremble, as did Millie and her two sisters, and the relief was tremendous when their father put the belt back in the drawer and said Tom was to be given one more chance. Her brother never had to have the belt administered. He was suitably deterred from wrongdoing.

# Chapter 7

Millie had been interested in hearing about the wall which had once surrounded Newcastle and wanted to know more about it. Arthur, her husband, said that he had learned a lot about the history of Newcastle from his mother Nellie and she might be able to help her. When Millie asked Nellie if she could tell her more about the Town Wall, Nellie was only too happy to oblige and show off her knowledge. She and Millie got together to talk about the wall. She certainly knew the subject well and Millie thought she was getting a history lesson.

Millie first asked a question: 'Why was it necessary to build a wall around Newcastle?'

'Well, Millie, Newcastle had enemies in medieval days. There were people who wanted to be powerful and own lots of land. They wanted to own our great town and tried to gain it by fighting for it and so there were many battles. Our main enemies were the Scots and in order to try and stop them, and any other enemies getting into our city, it was decided to surround the town with a very strong wall. It acted as a barrier for many years but as the years passed, the wall prevented our town growing and becoming richer by trading with other countries and so bit by bit the walls were demolished or fell into ruin.'

'I know that, Nellie, because I have seen some very well preserved bits of wall at Stowell Street, near where you live.'

'Quite right, Millie. I will take you one day to where there are more sections left of the old wall in Newcastle because there are quite a few. The wall was built in the 13th and 14th centuries and as I have already told you their main purpose was to defend the town against attack by invading Scottish armies and other military threats. Newcastle was frequently the assembly point for English troops preparing for expeditions north of the border, or to meet Scottish forces that had crossed into England. It was therefore an important military town as well as becoming an important centre of export trade, mainly for leather and wool in the middle ages. Coal did not become a major export until the 15th century.

'The constructing of the walls began during the reign of Edward the 1st in 1272 but took many years to build. They were largely complete by 1313, but the quayside wall was finished a little later because this area of Newcastle, called Sandhill, was densely populated. The reason for this was that in the 13th and 14th centuries the quayside and Sandhill were the centre of Newcastle and there were always obstacles in the way of building, not to mention the density of people who lived in the narrow, dirty streets and crowded buildings.

'The wall was very sturdy and well-built and I have always remembered the following piece of information I was given. During Henry VIII's reign the King's antiquarian John Leland described Newcastle's walls this way: 'The strength and magnificence of the walling of this town, far passeth all the walls of the cities of England and most of the towns of Europe'.'

'Did they surround the whole town, Nellie?'

'Oh yes. The wall, in its entirety, was a little over two miles long and was built from locally quarried stone. It was 10 feet thick and up to 30 feet high and it was possible to walk along the top of it. There were seven main fortified gates for access at key points of entry to the town, seventeen towers and a series of thirty turrets. Immediately inside the walls was a street so that you could walk right round the town, and ditches were even dug out next to the wall to add to its defence. The towers were semi-circular, on their outward looking side, and squared off on their town facing side. Loop holes were provided in the towers for arrows and the turrets in between the towers were mainly used as observation points. All the gates were locked at night, the most heavily fortified being the West Gate and New Gate, and the other five were Pilgrim Street Gate, Pandon Gate, Sand Gate, Close Gate and New Bridge Gate which was at the northern end of the Tyne Bridge and was actually the first to be completed. In addition to the fortified gates there were 17 'water' gates leading to the town quayside.

'There had of course to be some organisation if attacks on the town were to be held off and consequently Newcastle was divided into 24 districts and each of these was responsible for the defence of a particular gate or tower. The wall was well able to deal with attacks, especially from the Scots.'

'You were right, Nellie,' Millie interjected at this point. 'That wall was very well built.'

'Indeed it was and served its purpose admirably. As I have already said the civil war in 1644 was the last time the walls were attacked and after that they fell into disrepair.

'Now, just a word about the largest and strongest gate because it is relevant to the gallows. It was the New Gate and the town's gaol had been built into it. It was in use from 1400 until 1823. This was the gaol where the criminals were imprisoned before they were taken to the gallows to be hanged. It was not too far for them to walk from New Gate to Gallowgate.

'I have walked along Newgate Street many times to St. Andrew's church at Gallowgate and it is not a long walk, although the prisoners may have wished it was a bit longer when they were walking to their death. On the other hand they might have wished it was less of a walk so that the inevitable would be over as soon as possible. Who knows?

'When the New Gate prison closed because it was in such a state of disrepair, the thieves were moved to a new prison at Carliol Croft near Pilgrim Street and the debtors to a prison in the Castle Keep. The Newgate Prison, which had served Newcastle for centuries, was demolished in 1823.'

'Nellie, I have really enjoyed hearing that piece of history. You certainly enjoy acquiring knowledge. Arthur is just like you. I learn all sorts of things through him. Thank you.'

'I have enjoyed telling you, Millie. Now can I help you with anything else?'

'Well, not at the moment, Nellie, but I expect I will think of something in the future. I am going to have lots to tell the children that Arthur and I hope to have. Now I must go because I am meeting Arthur soon outside St. Andrew's Church. We are going for a walk to get some fresh air, but not too far, because we both have things to do tonight.'

# Chapter 8

When Millie met Arthur outside St. Andrew's church in Gallowgate they decided to walk along the road past 'The Strawberry' pub and perhaps call in there for a drink. This meant they were in the area of Gallowgate where there was still waste land but it was now a place, in 1882, where young lads and sometimes girls gathered to kick a ball around. There was certainly a growing interest in football and sometimes matches were arranged, which Arthur went to see. He said that he hoped one day Newcastle would have its own football team.

Some months after Millie's talk with Nellie about the walls and their first visit to 'The Strawberry' in 1882, Millie and Arthur became parents for the first time. They had two more children, one in 1884 and the other in 1886. They were kept busy while the children were growing up but Arthur still took an interest in football and often wheeled the pram round to the land where youngsters still kicked a ball around. He often stopped to watch them and 10 years later, in 1892, if Samuel, who was approaching 10 by then, was with him, he often joined the boys, kicking a ball around.

In 1892 football was beginning to be taken very seriously and there was talk of a town football club being formed. There were two football clubs by this time, one in the West end of Newcastle and one in the East end. It was decided in May 1892 that the two clubs would merge, to form Newcastle United, and this proved to be an excellent move. Crowds flocked to the home ground, St James' Park. This was the piece of ground which they had been given in Gallowgate by the council, to make a football pitch. It was not an ideal place because the land sloped badly with a drop of 18ft from North to South, but the land was eventually levelled and the footballers played their first season in 1893-4 in the football league Division 2. The club was not legally constituted as Newcastle United Football Club Co. Ltd until September 6th 1895. Arthur was delighted that Newcastle now had its own football team and if he possibly could, he attended every match.

He and Millie had taken all their children down to see the new football ground in 1892 and there was great excitement in Newcastle when it was fully realised that they had their very own football team. They were even prouder when, in the seasons from 1904 to 1911, they were league champions three times and cup winners in 1910.

Samuel used to go to watch football with his father but Millie never wanted to go. She enjoyed sewing and was quite happy to stay at home making clothes for her family. Sometimes while Arthur was with Samuel at the football ground, Millie took the children for a walk on the Town Moor. They loved running about on the wide open space. Grass could be seen for miles around and the air was fresh and clean. People took their dogs there for nice long walks and the children loved seeing the dogs also enjoying this massive area of unspoiled grassland in the middle of the town. Another delight for the children were the cows that grazed there.

Once, Rachel, their youngest daughter, had asked who looked after the cows because they should be on a farm so that the farmer could look after them. Millie had to explain that these were special cows owned by some special men called 'Freemen' and they were allowed to let their cattle graze on the Town Moor. She then had to assure Rachel and Esther that the cows were well looked after by the Freemen and she would tell them more about the Freemen when they were older, because they would understand better. They were just a little young to understand that the history of the Town Moor went back as far as Anglo-Saxon times when Anglo-Saxon 'free men' were a middle class breed of men, who carried arms for the defence of their community and because of their work were given special rights. Hence their cattle being allowed to graze on the moor.

Millie had all sorts of information which she could pass on to her children when they were older. Meanwhile, the great thing was that the Town Moor, which dates from at least 1357, is protected land and even though it is sought after by property developers it will always remain as grassland. Edward III granted a charter to Newcastle confirming possession of 89 acres of common land in 1357 but in the 20th century the total area of the Town Moor, flanked by Grandstand Road, Claremont Road and the Great North Road was 1,000 acres. Such an area of grassland in a city is rare and Millie told her children that Newcastle is very proud to have such a piece of land which is there for everyone to enjoy.

# Chapter 9

The years when the children were growing up were a delight to Millie and Arthur and they made the most of those years. That is why Millie always had happy memories which she could look back upon, which helped so much in the bad times and especially if she felt lonely. Well, she would not be lonely today, she thought to herself when she reached home that day of the big clean up. Her daughter Esther was coming round for tea with Sarah her granddaughter. Esther wanted to do some sewing on her mother's sewing machine.

She would just have to have a sit down first, with a cup of tea. She was really tired this morning after all that hard work and was glad to sit down in the lovely rocking chair that Arthur had made for her many years ago, when the children were small. She had rocked her babies to sleep on it many times. She loved it and would never ever part with it. She sat down and shook off her shoes before leaning back in the chair onto the little blanket that her daughter Rachel had made for her, when she was about twelve years of age. Rachel was a very sweet natured girl and very clever with her hands. Millie had taught her how to crochet and she had made lots of coloured squares and then sewn them together to make a soft blanket which fitted perfectly as a back rest on the rocking chair. Millie treasured it because Rachel, who had never been as strong as her siblings, Samuel and Esther, had died when she was only twenty years of age. Millie leaned back on the little blanket which always gave her comfort. She might allow herself a little snooze although she had quite a lot to do before Esther and Sarah arrived. She fell asleep thinking of her employer, Jack Riddell. He had been so nice to her this morning, apologising for the state of his pub and the amount of work there was to do. She liked him and he seemed to like her. She had never thought of any other man but Arthur, not even after he died, but she now found herself thinking how nice it would be to go out with Jack some time, as friends of course. Dear me, whatever was she thinking about at her age.

When she awoke there was just time for a quick dust, and time enough to make some scones for tea before she heard the familiar knock at the door and the sound of Sarah's voice shouting 'G R A N N Y'.

It was always a joy to have her granddaughter's company. She could always make her granny smile. She was such a chatterbox and had so much to tell about her day at school. Her words tumbled out of her mouth, sometimes without taking a breath and Millie always listened intently to what she had to say. She knew how important it was to listen and be interested in what children had to say. Sarah was 5 years of age in 1929, and had not been at school for very long but she loved it.

She asked endless questions and was interested in everything around her. It was obvious that she was an intelligent little girl and her teacher said she was a joy in the classroom because she was such a happy little girl, with an enquiring mind and a thirst for knowledge. Millie, Esther and Tom, her daddy, were so proud of her.

She was a bonny little girl with thick dark curls just like Samuel had had. In fact she reminded Millie of Samuel at that age because she was so good natured and full of life. Even her teeth were very white like his, which gave Sarah a lovely smile and she loved Granny's little saying about smiles. 'If you smile somebody else smiles and before you know it, you have miles and miles of smiles.'

Sarah told Millie that she had told her teacher about it and she had said it was a lovely thing to say and she would remember it forever. Sarah loved her teacher.

She was always hungry when she came home from school and enjoyed her tea, especially her granny's scones. 'They are delicious, Granny. Now what are we going to do now?'

'Well, I am going to sew, Sarah, so what do you want to do?' Esther asked her daughter.

'You and I could go to Leazes Park if you would like to,' Millie said. She always loved taking Sarah to Leazes Park. It was a very nice park and was actually the first public park in Newcastle. It had opened in December 1873, after a petition had been sent to the council, requesting them to provide some open ground for the purpose of health and recreation.

The park was designed around a lake and later a terrace and a bandstand had been added to it. Then in 1897 some beautiful gates were put up to commemorate the Diamond Jubilee of Queen Victoria. Millie had taken all her children down to the park to see the beautiful gates when they were put there and on returning home the two oldest children, Samuel and Esther, had made lovely pictures of them which she had stuck onto the kitchen wall. Children always liked to see their work on display so Millie had stuck the pictures onto the kitchen wall to show how much she valued them. They stayed up there for a long time because the children were so proud of them.

When they went to the park Sarah nearly always took a ball with her and loved to play games with it. Her favourite game was catchy but 'Piggy in the Middle' was another favourite, if both her mother and granny were with her. They had to keep well away from the lake of course when they were playing with the ball.

Now Sarah said, 'Granny, I am sorry but I do not want to go to the park tonight because I have something to show you and she took out of her little school bag a brand new skipping rope. 'I want to show you what I can do with it. Shall we go into the yard because I can show you better there?'

They went outside into the yard and Sarah began skipping.

'Very good, Sarah,' Millie said.

'Well, I used to catch my foot in the rope all the time at first but now I don't and I can do 50 jumps without stopping. Isn't that clever, Granny? And that is why Mother has bought me a brand new skipping rope, because I am getting very clever at using it. I love playing skippy ropes with my friends. My favourite game is 'higher and higher' but you really need three people, because two have to turn the rope. We have tried tying one end of the rope to the lamp-post but it does not work so well. My next favourite game is 'Calling in' but there has to be two or three playing it. One can skip while saying the rhyme 'I call in my very best friend and her name is… , whoever you choose to call in and that person comes to skip with you. It can be quite hard if there are two of you skipping in the same rope but I am getting better all the time. When one of you does catch their foot then you are out. Do you want to try it with me, Granny?'

'Well, another time because it is starting to rain. Let's go inside and find something else to do. We will skip next time you come.'

When they went inside Millie read a book to Sarah and then she got out the dolls that she kept at her house and together she and Sarah played with them. The dolls had lots of adventures before it was time to go home, but the doll that Sarah liked best was the one with a hard head but a soft body and she had to be very carefully put away in the little wooden bed which her daddy had specially made for her special doll. When she was older Granny was going to show Sarah how to knit because she wanted to make some new clothes for her special doll. Sometimes she took her special doll home to take to bed, together with her 'Raggy Teddy'. He was very special like her doll because he had once belonged to her Uncle Samuel, whom she had heard about but never seen. Granny had told Sarah that 'Raggy Teddy' was very precious and must be taken care of because he had to be there just in case Uncle Samuel ever came back home.

It was nearly time to go home when Sarah remembered something. 'Granny, I nearly forgot to mention it but have you remembered that 'The Hoppings' will be coming to the Town Moor very soon? Will you come with mother and myself like you did last year and the year before that?'

'I most certainly will, Sarah. I like 'The Hoppings' as much as you do because they bring back so many happy memories. We used to always go to 'The Hoppings' as a family when your mummy was a little girl and we loved it. It is sad that your grandfather, your Auntie Rachel and your Uncle Samuel are no longer able to come with us.'

'Granny, would you remind me again about Samuel, because your face always looks so sad when you say his name.'

'Well! He ran away I would think to London, Sarah, nearly twenty years ago and he never came back. We have not heard from him since. He would have loved you very much, Sarah, and you would have loved him. He was always such fun and he was always smiling, just like you.'

'Well, why has he not come back, Granny?' Sarah wanted to know.

'I cannot answer your question, Sarah, because I do not know the answer. I wish he would come home but he has never written a letter to me, since he went away. I do not even know whether he is still alive.'

'That is dreadful, Granny. Something serious must have happened for him to run away. I will wish and wish and wish that he comes home.'

'That would be a dream come true, Sarah.'

'Well,' Sarah continued, 'I wish I was a fairy godmother like the one in the Cinderella story and then I could wave a magic wand and make him come back. You would get such a wonderful surprise, wouldn't you?'

When it was time for her daughter and granddaughter to leave, there were always tears from Sarah. She loved going to her grandmother's and going home also meant going to bed. It was difficult to sleep sometimes, on the long, hot summer nights which they were having this year, and she hated lying in bed awake. She made bathtime last for ages on those nights and to waste more time she often used to pretend that she had got soap in her eyes, because then her mother had to spend ages getting it out. The stinging sensation seemed to go on for ages, or at least she made it be so, to maximise the sympathy and cuddle she used to get. If she was lucky there might just be a lovely sticky toffee to make her feel better.

On the night after her visit to Granny's, when she had reminded her about 'The Hoppings', Sarah fell asleep, dreaming about them and all the fun she would have on the roundabouts and swings. It was so good that Granny would be with them again.

After Esther and Sarah left it was not long before Millie climbed the stairs to bed, but despite her tiredness she did not go to sleep immediately. That was because Sarah had unwittingly evoked memories of happier times when her family was complete. In her mind she conjured up a picture of all her family, the people she loved most dearly. Arthur, Samuel, Esther, Rachel, Tom and Sarah and asked herself the question over and over: 'Where and why had it all gone wrong?'.

Then she remembered how excited Sarah was about going to 'The Hoppings' and she fell asleep thinking about Sarah and the lovely time she would have with her at the huge fair on the Town Moor. Perhaps this year she would pluck up the courage to go in a dodgem car again and be a better driver than she was last year. 'I hope the lovely weather stays until our visit' was her last thought before falling asleep.

The good weather stayed until their visit to the fair and as in other years they had a lovely time. Sarah shouted and screamed with delight on all the rides. The faster the ride the happier she was and this year Millie did much better on the dodgem cars. They hardly bumped into anybody and Millie actually enjoyed it and was proud of her steering skills. Last year she had vowed never to go in a dodgem car again because she felt so sick and dizzy but she never refused Sarah anything, if she could help it and Sarah pleaded with her to brave the dodgems again. Somehow Sarah could get her to do anything!

'The Hoppings' as they were called, was actually a very large travelling fair which came to Newcastle once a year for a week and was held on the Town Moor. It was very popular and there was some interesting history attached to it.

It had begun with horse racing which took place regularly on the Town Moor in the 18th and early 19th century and the 'Newcastle Races' was a big event which was extremely popular. There was entertainment of all kinds, beer tents, side shows, and even cock-fighting, and a grandstand was erected in 1800, making it even more of a grand occasion.

There was, however, a lot of dubious behaviour and a great deal of alcohol was drunk. It was becoming a very rowdy event. Millie recalled one night when she was very young and her father had come home very drunk after attending the races and her mother had slapped his face hard. They had not spoken to one another for a whole week and Millie had fretted terribly because she thought her father was going to leave them. He did not come home drunk ever again.

Things changed when the Grandstand committee bought an estate in Gosforth, from the Brandling family and the 'Newcastle Races' week was moved there and a permanent grandstand was erected.

To mark the change, a different festival came to the Town Moor, in the same place where the races had been held. It was called 'The Temperance Festival' and one of its objectives was to show people that you could have a good time without drinking yourself silly. There were no alcoholic drinks, although non-alcoholic drinks were set out in front of the old grandstand. A number of platforms were also set up for speakers, warning the crowd of all the perils of alcohol.

The Temperance festival, however, gradually became much more fun with roundabouts and swings and sideshows, all of which could be enjoyed by the whole family and eventually it was given a new title 'The Hoppings'.

By the time Sarah was taken there, there were lots of roundabouts, swings and stalls and she loved them all. There were all sorts of rides when she could squeal to her heart's content and laugh and giggle at all sorts of things. Every year it seemed to get better, especially the food. The stickier her hands got with the candy floss, toffee apples and ice cream cornets, the better. There was a smile on everyone's face when the Hoppings were on and it got bigger and better every year. Sarah loved trying her luck at the various stalls, her favourite being 'hook a duck'. One year her gran had hooked one for her and she had carried that little duck everywhere with her.

Sarah wanted to know one day how the event got the funny name of 'The Hoppings'. Millie was not terribly sure but one theory was that at the end of each day, after all the work of the day was done, the people who owned the roundabouts, swings and stalls, and any visitors who were still loitering, gathered together to feast and drink and then dance or hop around a bonfire to the music of local pipers or fiddlers, and so the name Hoppings was chosen for the festival instead of the more mundane title of Temperance Festival.

Samuel, their beloved son, had, like Sarah, adored going to 'The Hoppings'. He loved speed and the faster the rides were the better he liked it. There was usually a wrestling booth at 'The Hoppings' and Samuel, who loved all sport, enjoyed getting involved in that but his main sport was rowing. This had become a passion in Newcastle, towards the end of the 19th century. The River Tyne was the perfect place for it as it had a long history of watermen, going right back to the keelmen. The first ever Tyne Rowing Regatta was held in 1834 and from it grew a tremendous cult, with its own heroes, legends and songs. A top rower then would be idolised by everyone.

Millie was never interested in hearing about rowing. Samuel had been a rower but had never rowed again after that dreadful accident on the last Rowing Regatta he had attended. In fact she blamed that accident for changing their lives so dramatically and talking about rowing always brought back sad and bad memories of Samuel.

Samuel was their first child and their only son and though she loved all her children with a fierce protective love, she had to admit to herself that her son was adored, even more than his sisters. She often wondered if that was why he had been taken from them, and she and Arthur were being punished for having a favourite child? Arthur had absolutely adored his one and only son.

'Samuel' they had called him. Her mother told them that it was a biblical name, but Millie did not know that because unlike her mother she had never read a Bible. She remembered her grandmother once showing her a huge, very old, very thick book with well-worn pages and she had told Millie it was their family Bible and all the names of their family were written in the front of it. She showed Millie where her name was printed.

Sometimes Millie took the children to a service at St. Andrew's church and she had had them baptised there but the services were not really for children and the children got bored quickly and started fidgeting. She worried about them disturbing other people and in the end she stopped going, but she very often called in at St Andrew's church, if she was walking down Gallowgate into town to do her shopping. She enjoyed the quietness of the church and she also liked to reflect about things. She imagined God all around her but she did not fully understand about Him. It was difficult to address Someone you could not see although she understood that Faith was believing God was there. One thing she always did was thank God for Arthur, her husband, and her three lovely children, Samuel, Esther and Rachel.

Samuel their firstborn gave them joy from the moment he was born. He was such a happy and contented baby, who always had a smile for everyone. He was described by his teachers as being a very bright little boy who would go far. The teachers loved him and he was popular with the other schoolchildren and Millie and Arthur were so proud of him. He grew into a very handsome young man and had an easy charm and the gift of knowing what to say in any situation. The curly hair of his baby days had lengthened to curl neatly into the nape of his neck but Samuel found his hair irksome. It was too curly and he battled with it daily to keep it under control. He used to hate it when his mother tried to brush it. He suffered many sharp knocks on the head and cries of, 'Keep still, Samuel, please'. How could he be still when it was hurting so much?

Millie could not help smiling when she thought of the hair of her daughters, Esther, and Rachel. Their hair was very, very straight. She used to try in vain to make it curlier by tearing up sheets into long white rags, which she then wound around thick strands of hair, to make ringlets, but usually all her efforts were in vain. Oh dear! Samuel used to make fun of his sisters when they sat with their rags in and that used to infuriate them and they would then try to find ways to tease him.

One day they thought of a perfect way. Samuel was very particular about his name. He insisted that everyone call him by his full name. No-one must shorten it. He would not tolerate being called Sam or Sammy. Samuel sounded much more distinguished and that was what he must be called. It made him furious when his sisters began calling him Sam one day and Sammy the next. They giggled and giggled when he got angry and they said they would only cease when he stopped giggling at them in their hair rags. A truce was called and much to Millie and Arthur's relief the teasing stopped, although every now and then if they got angry with one another they teased again, but it was very light hearted banter. Both parents felt it was good for siblings to disagree at times and it helped them not to take themselves too seriously. Good natured banter was good for a family and certainly the children grew up to respect their parents and one another.

# Chapter 10

A young man was standing up in the train as it approached the city of Newcastle. He felt a quiver of excitement run through him but a glimmer of apprehension too. It was twenty years since he had left the town where he had been born and where he had been brought up. Queen Victoria had died in 1901, and he had left Newcastle in 1909. He had left it in anger, with hate and loathing in his heart, but he did not want to think about that at this moment in time so he pushed those niggles about his return to one side. He could not help wondering, however, if his family were still alive as he had made no contact with them at all, during his long absence. He could not help feeling a little guilty about this but he had felt it best to sever all ties with them at that time.

The train was sweeping down that big curve from Gateshead to Newcastle, where it crossed the River Tyne, which meant he was almost home. There had been a major change since he had left all those years ago. A new bridge had been built over the River Tyne. Samuel loved bridges and he remembered so well all that his father had told him about the bridges that crossed the River Tyne. He would have to find out the details of this new bridge.

His father may not even be alive now and in any case he had no desire to contact him again, so he would have to find the information elsewhere. It had been good when he was a boy and when he was so close to his father, who had worked on the docks and was very knowledgeable about the quayside. As a lad of thirteen years old he had often gone to meet his father from work and enjoyed so much conversation with him as they walked home. Despite his resentment of his father now, he always got a warm feeling when he thought back to those times. He had learnt so much from his father and he had loved learning about the bridges.

His father had told him that a bridge, built by the Romans, had spanned the River Tyne since at least the 2nd century, although the exact spot is not absolutely certain. A new bridge was built across the Tyne in 1248, on what is thought to have been the site of the first Roman bridge. It is thought to have had 12 arches. It was defended by three towers and on it towards the southern end was the Blue Stone which marked the boundary between Newcastle and the Palatinate of Durham. This bridge was still in existence until 1771. Over time a number of buildings were erected on the bridge itself, some on one side and some straddled across the whole bridge with arches through them to allow access. Most of them were built over the supporting piers but there were some which extended over the river on timber supports. On the Newcastle side there was even a little chapel built dedicated to St. Thomas-a-Becket, Archbishop of Canterbury, who was murdered in Canterbury Cathedral on the 29th December 1170.

Samuel used to try and picture the bridge in his mind and decided that he would have liked to live on that bridge and every morning come out onto it and look down at the water flowing under the bridge, making its way to the mouth of the river at Tynemouth. Somehow it appealed to his sense of adventure, to think of the vast ocean which awaited the river to take it away to other lands. He once said this to his father and he said, 'Well now, son, you would not like to have been living on that bridge in 1771, because the River Tyne flooded and on Sunday 17th November, a number of the arches collapsed and by December7th, there was very little left of the houses built on the Gateshead side of the bridge because they had collapsed into the river. Six people were killed, including a shopkeeper and his shop assistant. There is actually a rather sad story attached to that shopkeeper.'

'Tell me about it, Father,' said Samuel, 'you know how I love stories.'

'Well,' his father replied, 'the shop assistant had forgotten something and told the shopkeeper that she must go back to retrieve it. He told her she must not do that as they had been lucky to escape from the shop and must get off the bridge as quickly as possible but the silly girl took no notice of the warning. She went back and was swept away in the flood because the arch beneath their shop collapsed at the very moment she went back into it. Let that be a lesson to you, Samuel: you should always respect the advice of an older person because they are usually wiser; and by the way nineteen houses survived the flood on the Newcastle side but of course they all suffered structural damage. I heard that all the bridges built across the River Tyne at that time were all swept away, except for one at Corbridge which is a small town further up the river.'

'What happened next, Father?' Samuel wanted to know.

'Well, son, they had to build another bridge, which was known as the Georgian Bridge and it took six years to build. A temporary bridge had to be put in place in 1772, utilising as much of the old medieval bridge as possible, but the new bridge was attractively built in stone with nine arches, with a decorative balustrade over them. It was opened in 1781 but the arches were still very low and only small boats could get through them. This was becoming a problem because, with growing trade in Newcastle and industry developing along the river, the bridge was becoming an obstruction, as it prevented large boats passing up the river to collect cargo and get it back to the mouth of the River Tyne.'

'Father, I just want to ask if they built houses on the new Georgian bridge?'

'No, son, not this time. It was not really a good idea and they did not want another disaster. You see, Samuel, people were learning a lot of new skills and were becoming more and more creative, which means they were having lots of new ideas to make things, which were attractive as well as being useful.

'Now as I have already told you, the Georgian Bridge within a century was recognised as a serious obstacle to the prosperity of the River. You see I said that people were becoming increasingly creative and there were new developments in industry. Rivers were very useful for carrying things by boat to places, especially if they were big and clumsy. This presented a problem because only the smallest boats could pass under the bridges over the River Tyne. The boats which could easily pass under were those of the keelmen. Now, Samuel, I am going to ask you to ask your Grandma about the keelmen because they were quite important people on Tyneside and your grandfather had a relative who was a keelman, so the next time you go to your grandmother's, ask her about her Uncle Frederick. I can tell you, though, that the Georgian Bridge eventually had to be pulled down. It was replaced at first by a wooden bridge and then much later by the Tyne Swing Bridge, which opened in 1876.'

'Were their arches on the swing bridge, Father?'

'Definitely not, Samuel. What do you think was going to be essential for the new bridge?'

'Well, it would have to be high enough this time for the big ships to go under it.'

'That is right, son, but how were they going to do that? Remember I told you that people were learning new skills and especially in the building trade. They had great new ideas and could design machinery which was so useful to builders and designers. They were called engineers and Newcastle was very fortunate in having some very clever engineers, who lived and worked in the town and the surrounding area, in the 19th century.

One of them was a man called Armstrong, and, Samuel, it was this William Armstrong who set up the engineering works at Elswick, which as you know is where I work. He had a very clever idea. He designed a swivel technique so that the bridge could swing open to let big ships travel up and down the river. These big ships travelled to other countries, so that coal and other goods could be sold to them, which was a way of trading, and this in turn helped to make our country rich. It was really very clever of William Armstrong to devise such a clever, swivel device called an hydraulic crane so that the bridge could swing open.'

'No wonder it was called the Swing Bridge,' Samuel commented. 'And when was it opened, Father?'

'In 1876, son, and what a difference it made to the river.'

Samuel always listened carefully to what his father had to say and he was particularly interested in the engineers his father told him about. The idea of being an engineer appealed to him. He wanted to invent something like William Armstrong. His father obviously admired Mr Armstrong immensely and he wanted his father to admire him and be proud of him. It would be wonderful if he could, one day, be a very clever, famous engineer.

One of the men who sometimes walked home with Arthur and Samuel told them that there was a blind man who could be seen every day on the Swing Bridge, at exactly the same place. He was said to be standing in the centre of the bridge which indicated the boundary between Newcastle and Gateshead and therefore he was avoiding the authorities, and no-one could remove him from that spot.

'Well why would he do that?' said Samuel. 'It seems silly to me. I wonder if he slept there. Surely not because he would get very cold through the night especially in the winter. I wonder why he did it?'

'Well,' Arthur replied, 'perhaps in his mind he was the guardian of the bridge and it made him feel important, or perhaps he felt safe there because if he was blind, walking about would be difficult for him. I don't think he was wanting people to give him money and I agree that it was a strange thing to do. No one will ever know why he did it. Anyway he was found one day collapsed in the snow after some severe weather and he died of pneumonia, or so the story goes.'

'Poor, poor man!' Samuel said. 'Someone should have been looking after him and fancy not being able to see. I would hate that more than anything. I think of all the senses, that is the one which is worst of all.'

'Father, will you tell me more about William Armstrong. He was obviously a very clever, interesting man?' Samuel said.

'There is quite a lot to tell, Samuel. We will wait until after supper and then sit down and I will tell you all about him.'

That evening his father was true to his word and after their evening meal he and Samuel settled down for a good long talk about Lord William Armstrong, who was an iconic figure in the history of Newcastle.

'He was born on November the 26th in 1810 in Shieldfield, a suburb in the east end of Newcastle and was named William after his father, who was a wealthy and knowledgeable man, and a keen member of the Literary and Philosophical Society of Newcastle upon Tyne. This society had been formed to promote science and the advancement of knowledge, and although his main interest was mathematics he was very interested in science and educating people to be interested in acquiring knowledge.

'William senior's son William was not a healthy child. He had to spend a lot of time indoors and to occupy himself he began making toy machines, which he loved doing, using all kinds of different materials. He apparently loved to visit the workshop of a local joiner so that he could learn about the tools he used in his trade. Another place he loved to visit and where he spent a good deal of time, was Rothbury in Northumberland, because his family felt the Northumbrian air was good for him and he certainly loved that area.

'As he grew older his enthusiasm for mechanics increased and he spent time at William Ramshaw's Engineering works based in Bishop Auckland. It was this town in County Durham where he was sent to school in 1826 when he was 16. William's ambition was to be an engineer or a scientist, but his father had other ideas for him. He wanted his son to be a lawyer and arranged for him to train under a personal friend of his, but he could not stifle the love his son had for mechanics and all of his leisure pursuits were to do with mechanics. Whenever possible he loved to visit a factory in the high bridge area of Newcastle which made clocks and telescopes and other mechanical items. He watched keenly to see how they were made.

'He also enjoyed fishing and it was during one of his fishing expeditions that he became fascinated with the idea of water as a source of power, having seen an old water wheel in action. He actually drew up plans for a rotary engine powered by water and the device was built at the factory of Henry Watson, the very factory he had visited many times as a young man. No businessman took up the invention but William continued to develop his water powered ideas. He developed a plan for a hydraulic crane and in around 1845 he converted a crane on Newcastle's Quayside to water power.

You can see now how he eventually came to build The Swing Bridge, in the 1870s. As a result of the efficiency of the crane he had invented he left his job as a solicitor and opened a factory at Elswick for the production of his cranes and other hydraulic equipment. The Elswick Works went on to enjoy many years of success and became Newcastle's largest employer.

'In 1884 Tyneside was becoming world renowned for its shipbuilding industry and a ship yard was opened at Elswick. In fact, Samuel, although I was not aware of it at the time, even though I was working there, I was told later that in 1895 11,000 men and boys worked there and that when a big order came in there could be as many as 13,000 of us working on site. The latter of course was growing all the time. It began as five acres of land and now it is 50 acres and stretches along the Northern bank of the River Tyne for nearly three quarters of a mile. .

'Elswick was once a very small suburb of Newcastle, Samuel, in the west end of Newcastle but it has become an industrial empire with William Armstrong at its head. I am very proud to be working there.

'There is even more to his story because in the 1850s, before his building of the Swing Bridge, William branched out into arms production and shipbuilding and developed a breech loading mobile field gun for use during that decade. He was knighted in 1859, the year your mother was born, and his company went on to produce naval guns and warships.'

'Where did William Armstrong live, Father, when he was grown up because if he was so rich and successful he must have lived in an expensive house?'

'Yes, Samuel, he was a rich man but he was not greedy. He used a lot of his money to help other people, as you will see. He had built a home close to Jesmond Dene, in the east end of Newcastle and had commissioned the building of a banqueting hall on the western side of Jesmond Dene where he entertained guests. That was completed in 1862.

'Remember I told you that William was delicate as a young child and was taken to Rothbury many times so that he could benefit from the fresh Northumbrian air. Well he loved the countryside around Rothbury and decided this was where he wanted to build a country house, for himself and his wife. It would be a house where they could entertain their many friends, very lavishly.

'Work began on his country mansion in 1864 at Cragside, close to Rothbury and it was built on a very craggy hillside, because he found that location interesting. He created wonderful grounds by planting thousands of trees and shrubs. A great many of these were rhododendrons and the house became well known for these beautiful shrubs. The grounds were very like the slopes of Jesmond Dene, where he had also planted wonderful plants and trees.

'Your mother and I walked in Jesmond Dene many times when we were younger and we must go there sometime with your mother and sisters. We will have to get a tram to take us because it is quite a long way from here. There are some lovely walks and woodland paths beside the River Ouseburn which runs through the dene. I will be able to show you the house and Banqueting Hall that he built there.

I am told that Sir Armstrong's mansion at Rothbury was extended many times and its interior was redesigned a number of times, and lavishly furnished so that he and his wife entertained in a very grand style. They even entertained Royalty and it is said that when they had Prince Edward V11th and Princess Alexandra, descendants of Queen Victoria, staying with them, the grounds were strewn with lovely Chinese Lanterns. It must have been a lovely sight.

'However, the main thing to remember about that house, Samuel, is that it was the first house in the world to be wholly lit by hydro-electricity, which I suppose is not too surprising considering William Armstrong's great interest in hydro water power. The location of the house, remember, was chosen because it was interesting. He had the idea right at the beginning to explore hydro electricity.

'Now we come to what I think is the best the best bit of Mr Armstrong's story. I told you he was a very rich man but also a very kind one and he never forgot the people who worked in his factories because they had been instrumental in him becoming wealthy and successful. He owed a great deal to the workers and managers at his factory in Elswick and he wanted to put money back into the communities. He and his wife, who unfortunately had no children of their own, supported many charities during their lifetime in the North East and particularly in Newcastle, and as I have already told you, gave Jesmond Dene to the people of Newcastle, which they appreciate very much. It really is a lovely place to walk in, which is why we must go sometime.

"Lord Armstrong, for that is his title, is definitely a very special man, Samuel. He was knighted in 1859 which gave him the title of Sir William Armstrong and then in 1887, the year of Queen Victoria's Golden Jubilee, he was raised to the peerage as Baron Armstrong of Cragside, which meant that for the last three years of his life he was addressed as Lord William Armstrong. They say that he is as enthusiastic about his work as ever."

Samuel was to recall the conversation he had had with his father, several years later, in 1900. He was at college when he learnt that Lord William Armstrong had died at the age of 90 on the 27th of December, at his home in Rothbury and had been buried on December 31st 1900, in Rothbury Parish Church.

'Father, I have really enjoyed hearing about William Armstrong but you won't forget that you are going to tell me about the other famous bridge of the River Tyne, The High Level Bridge.'

'I won't forget, Samuel, but that is enough for tonight.'

# Chapter 11

It was several weeks later before Arthur had the opportunity to tell his son about the other bridge built over the river and it was a very special one.

'That was because the man who designed it was another very clever man. Tyneside produced some very clever men, Samuel, of whom we can be very, very proud. This man was called a genius by many people. His name was Robert Stephenson, and he was the son of George Stephenson who was famous for building the first Steam Locomotive Engine. There is so much you should know about the Stephenson family and their pioneering work in the field of steam engines but we will have to leave it until another day. It is a fascinating story. I think you are beginning to see, Samuel, that there is so much to learn about the world in which we live and I want you to work hard at school so that you will be clever and when you are grown up I am sure there will be many opportunities open to you to do exciting things, even travel round the world. Now back to the bridge.

'The High Level Bridge was constructed between 1845 and 1849 and was built for the York, Newcastle and Berwick railway. It was the first major example of a wrought iron, bow string girder bridge, which provided a double deck with rail traffic on the top level and road traffic on the lower deck. In fact, Samuel, it was the first bridge to be built like that in the world. How amazing is that!

The wonderful thing is that it was built on Tyneside, something of which we can be very, very proud.

'Apparently nineteen design ideas were submitted for a design for the High Level Bridge but the design of Robert Stephenson and Thomas Harrison was the design chosen. You see, Samuel, a new age was beginning. The age of 'Steam' which in turn led to a whole new age. This was the age of the train and railways developed rapidly, firstly throughout Britain and then the rest of the world. I think that is enough for now, Samuel, as we are nearly home.'

'No, Father, there is just time to tell me a little more about the High Level Bridge. We still have to walk up past St. Andrew's church where you said you and Mother were married.'

'Well, son, as I have said the age of steam and train was beginning in the 1840s, and that is why more bridges over rivers were necessary. Trains were a much faster way to travel but the trains that travelled north from London could get no further than Gateshead. Why do you think that was, Samuel?'

Samuel did not have to think for long. 'It is obvious, Father. Trains need rails and rails cannot be laid in a river, so no train would ever be able to cross a river.'

'Good, son. When a train travelled from London it had to stop at Gateshead and the passengers had to cross the river somehow and go to the station in Newcastle to get on another train to Scotland or some other place on that side of the river. Apparently, Samuel, there was a very shallow part of the river, near to where the old Roman bridge had been and it was possible to walk across the river if you knew the place, but this was not an ideal situation. It was obvious that a bridge would have to be built but it would have to be high because the River Tyne had very steep sides, and there could be no risk of the bridge not being high enough above the river. George Stephenson was a very clever railway engineer and he had built the first steam train. It was his son Robert who designed the High

Level Bridge so that trains could cross the river and this made a direct link from London to Edinburgh.'

'When was the bridge finished, Father?'

'It was finished in 1849 so it had taken four years to complete. Not surprising really because there was a tremendous amount of work involved in its construction. It is 112 feet high and a series of cast iron arches spring from massive granite piers embedded in the river. The bridge was opened by our very own Queen Victoria, who as you know was Queen of England for 64 years. She was married as you know to Prince Albert who very sadly died in 1861, when he was only 41. I have been told that the Queen and Prince Albert were returning from Scotland where they had been on holiday and the train in which they were travelling stopped on the bridge and Queen Victoria did not even get out of the train to declare the bridge open and so there was no special ceremony for its opening.

'Apparently the Queen did say that she and Prince Albert were very interested in the bridge, particularly because it was the first of its kind in the world. A great crowd had gathered on the river banks to watch the opening ceremony and of course to see the Queen and Prince Albert, so they must have been very disappointed, don't you think, Samuel?'

'I do, Father,' Samuel replied. 'I wonder why she did that because it was an honour for our country to be the designer and builder of the first bridge of its kind in the world. The Queen should have been so proud. I think people are strange sometimes.'

'Well we will never know why she did it and we are nearly home, so that is all for today but tomorrow on our way home we will go to the bridge and you can get a good look at it and even stand on it.'

The next evening Arthur kept his word and took his son to the site of the bridge with a view to walking across it. Samuel found it very exciting walking across the bridge, knowing that a train could be travelling above his head. One day he wanted to travel on a train that crossed the River Tyne. Meanwhile he enjoyed looking at the river from both sides of the bridge. It must have been very hard work indeed to make such a huge double decker bridge.

When Samuel got home that night after his visit to the bridge he asked if he could walk round to his grandmother's house because she just lived in the next street. 'Why do you want to go there, son. It is getting late?' his mother said.

'Well,' replied Samuel, 'I remember her once saying to me that she had gone to the opening of the High Level Bridge, and I would like to know more about that.'

Gran did not disappoint him. 'Yes, Samuel, I did go to the opening of that bridge, and I was so excited about it. Your granddad and I went down to the quayside on the 15th August 1849 when the first passenger train crossed the bridge. It was sent across the bridge from Gateshead while cannons fired and we all held our breath in case it toppled into the river below. On September 28th we had to go back again when Queen Victoria officially opened the bridge. We tried but we could not see the Queen because she did not leave the train in which she was travelling from Scotland. Many people were disappointed that day. I had put on my very best dress for the occasion. I loved that dress and I can still hear my mother saying to me, "Ellen, you look real bonny today in that outfit." The latter was in true Victorian style, a long skirt made with beautiful thick material and a matching jacket which had a peplum around the waist. I wore a small hat with a feather on the side and a pair of leather gloves which covered my wrists and stretched some way up my arm. I felt really grand, Samuel, and do you know what your grandad said? He said, "You look like a queen yourself, Nellie. Fancy me having my own Queen!" That was such a lovely thing to say and it made me feel like a queen, Samuel. I had a smile on my face all day long after that.'

'Thank you, Grandma, for telling me all about that day. It does seem strange to me that the King and Queen did not leave the train.

'Please could I come back another day after school because my father said you could tell me all about keelmen?'

'I would love to tell you about keelmen, Samuel, so come back another day and make it soon. I love the river and I love walking along the quayside. I am proud to be a Geordie, Samuel. Newcastle is a great city which is becoming very important. Some very clever men live in this city, and I want you to work hard at school, listen well to your teachers so that when you are grown up you will be clever. Your father is a clever man and knowledgeable about many things as you have been finding out recently and he wants you to learn new things and, who knows, one day you might be famous yourself.

'The schools are getting so much better. When I was a little girl schools were few and far between and a good education was not easy to acquire. Snow Street, which you attend, is a good school and you must make the most of it. When I go down by the quayside where your father works I see signs of industry everywhere. There is talk of ships being built on Tyneside and that will certainly be to our city's advantage. Just being made a city in 1882 has given Newcastle added status and if shipbuilding becomes an industry on Tyneside the area will become an important and prosperous place to be, by the time you have grown up. Ship building would not have been possible at one time because the River Tyne presented a huge problem. Do you know what it was?'

'Well I think I do, Gran, because my father has told me that the River Tyne presents a difficulty for big ships to come up it and only the keelboats of the Keelmen can get up the river easily.'

'You are so right, Samuel. Good lad. Now here I have baked some fresh bread today, so I will give you some to take home to your mother. She has always loved my freshly baked loaves. It will be a treat for her.'

'Thanks, Gran,' said Samuel. 'I love your bread too. We all do and teatime will be special today, especially if mother has baked some of her pies as well. I'll be back very soon to hear about the keelmen.'

'I can tell you a lot about them, Samuel, because my uncle was a keelman and they were important people on the river but that is for another day. Off you go home now; your mother will be wondering where you are.'

# Chapter 12

The next day after school Samuel did not go to meet his father, he went to Grandmother's again. He knew she loved him to go and she was such a good teller of things whether it was stories or information and he couldn't wait to hear about the keelmen of Newcastle. 'Who were they, Gran?'

'They were a group of men who worked on the river. They sailed the boats which were called keels and which carried coals down the river to the sea where they were loaded onto big sea going ships called colliers, which then took the coals to other parts of the world. Samuel, I am sure you are learning about the mines and coalfields at school, so you will know that there are many coal mines in Northumberland and Durham and it is a valuable commodity that other countries want. It is called exporting and in the same way we take in commodities from other countries which is called importing. Trading as it is called with other countries builds up wealth and our very own town of Newcastle is becoming more prosperous. You will have noticed when you go to meet your father from work that there are many dirty, dilapidated houses down by the river which will have to be demolished and the area will have to be made more desirable. Some people are living in very unsatisfactory conditions but if our town is getting richer there may be more money to spend on improving people's living conditions. Now back to the keelmen, Sam.'

'Samuel, you mean, Grandma. Not just Sam, remember?'

'I think your father will have told you about the problem on the River Tyne.'

'Yes, I know that it was a difficult river to navigate because it was twisty and shallow in parts and silted up in others and I know big ships could not get right up the river because the bridges were too low. This meant that smaller boats had to take any cargo to the mouth of the river in order to load onto the big ships.'

'Good boy, Samuel, you have been listening hard to your father. You are so like him when he was a young boy. He always asked a lot of questions and loved getting facts about things. Sometimes your grandad and I could not answer all his questions. However, I can answer your questions today, about the keelmen. You are right about the big ships getting up the river. They had to sail out to sea from Tynemouth or South Shields. This meant that smaller boats would have to take the goods to the big ships and that is where the keelmen come in. Their boats were called keel boats and the men who sailed them were called keelmen. That makes sense, doesn't it? The boats were specially made so that they could collect the coal, which had been brought across land to the river, and then take it down the River Tyne to Tynemouth or South Shields, to be loaded onto big ships. The boats were made from wood, low and flat-bottomed, and were 40 ft long and at least 19 ft wide, so they were very broad. They had a single mast with a square sail attached to them with a yard arm and two large oars. Each keel was manned by a skipper, two crewmen and a boy. These boats of course could easily get between the arches of the old Tyne bridge and could not get stuck on the sand banks at the sides of the river. The current of the river carried them up to the sea and they could use a sail if necessary. The incoming tide helped them to get back up the river. The keelmen had to load the boats, which could actually hold 16 tons of coal, so you can see, Samuel, that it was very hard work. Coal, of course, is a very valuable commodity, and had been exported from the River Tyne since the thirteenth century. Today it is still of great importance, particularly in industry.

'The keelmen of the River Tyne were very proud of the work they did and formed a very close knit community. Sometimes there was not enough work for them, due to the weather or supply of coal from the pits and so there were hard times for some of them.

'They were known as aggressive, hard drinking, swearing men but when dressed for an occasion they looked very distinctive in blue jackets, yellow waistcoats, bell bottom trousers and blue bonnets. My uncle looked ever so great when he had on his 'going out' clothes. My auntie put up with a lot, though, from my uncle because he would work all day long on the keelboats and then come home drunk in the evenings, and he did nothing to help with the children. Added to that they lived in the Sandgate area of Newcastle which was certainly not a very nice part of Newcastle. The streets were smelly and dirty with rubbish thrown everywhere and the sanitation was extremely poor. It was near to the river where the industry was, which made it dark and noisy. Every year my aunt seemed to be expecting a baby and in the end had thirteen children. Somehow she managed to bring them all up with little help from her husband, but she actually wore herself out and died when she was 45 years of age, which is not really very old.

'My uncle lived on for a long time, always in the hope that his sons would keep up the tradition of keelmen, which was that the trade was passed down from father to son. The other children more or less brought up each other and I am sorry to say often slept rough in the streets – imagine that. I am ashamed that that could happen in our family.

'Now, Samuel, I think that is enough information for today. You can come back another day but before you go you are going to have some of the broth I have made today. It is very good for you and will help to make good bones so that you grow up to be really strong. Now sit down and get that down you but before you sup it say thank you to God because He it was who created the world and gave us the land to grow crops so that we will never be hungry. There are parts of the world where people are hungry because their crops fail often and cannot provide food for them. Even in Newcastle there are children who beg on the streets because they are hungry. You just have to walk along the quayside to see poor children, so do as I say and thank God that you have food to eat and clothes to wear and shoes on your feet.'

Samuel was quite thoughtful while he was drinking his broth, because Grandmother had given him a lot to think about, and he did not forget to thank Grandmother when he finished her tasty broth.

The very next day Samuel was back at his grandmother's after school wanting more information about keelmen. 'Well there is something quite important and I am going to take you to see it one of these days, Sam.'

'Samuel, Gran. Don't forget – you said Sam.'

'The keelmen were not rich but they worked very hard and they were thrifty and decided in 1699 that they wanted to build a hospital or residential home for elderly, sick and disabled keelmen, and widows of keelmen and they wanted to build it and pay for it themselves. The Newcastle Corporation gave them a piece of land near Sandgate, on which to build and so they had four pence per keel journey deducted from their wages and building their hospital began. It was completed in 1701. They called it 'The Keelman's Hospital'; it had 50 rooms built round a central courtyard. It had cost £2000 to build and of course the keelmen were very proud of it. I remember my uncle going on and on about it when I was a little girl, Samuel. We used to get really fed up. My mother said we were always raising our eyebrows to each other to show our boredom and dislike of him. My uncle had seven sons and my mother said that before he died he made each of his sons promise to carry on the tradition of fathers handing down their trade to their sons. The sons each became keelmen and worked well into the 19th century, after which there was a severe drop in the necessity for the keel boats and by the end of the century they had ceased to be used on the River Tyne.'

'Why was that?' Samuel wanted to know.

'Well, things were changing,' Gran replied. 'In 1750 coal mines were being sunk further and further away from the river and coals were being brought to the riverside by wagon ways, which at first were horse drawn wagons but later were steam driven and could travel on rails right out in the river by the staithes which were being built. They were short pier like structures which projected out over the river.

'Then in 1787 more coal mines had opened nearer the mouth of the river and so more collier ships could sail up the river at high tide to load coal directly into their holds. This was not good news for the keelmen. It was a threat to their livelihood. And, of course, that is what happened Samuel and you will not see a keel boat again on the River Tyne.

'The state of the River Tyne was increasingly becoming an issue and it was obvious that money must be spent on it. So it was that in 1861 a long term programme of intensive dredging began that deepened the channel. Sand and mudbanks, shallows and other obstructions to navigations were begun. With the river now widened, straightened, and deepened, it was now much easier for ships to journey up the river and load their cargo directly at the staithes.

'Now, Samuel, do you think you know enough about the keelmen now?'

'Yes, Gran, but I think the keelmen should always be remembered because they did a good job for the city in their day.'

'I quite agree, son,' said Gran.

That evening Arthur finished the story of the ships by telling his son that the scene on the river had changed greatly in the 19th century. 'The shipbuilding industry had begun on Tyneside and Newcastle was to become famous for its shipbuilding. Bigger ships were now able to get further up the river. The decision had been made to take down the old Tyne Bridge with its 12 arches because it was a hindrance in that ships could not pass under its arches. I know you have heard all about the High Level Bridge and the old Tyne Bridge and I have even told you about the Swing Bridge which replaced the old Tyne Bridge. We will have to pay another visit to the quayside bridges and have a good look at them, because they have played quite a big part in the history of Newcastle.

'It is Friday tomorrow, the end of the week, so we will have a bit more time when you meet me from work. We will go when you come to meet me.'

# Chapter 13

Looking back now as he reminisced, Samuel realised that it was that Friday, that marked the beginning of the secret that was to have such an affect on his life. When Samuel went to meet his father the next evening it was very different. His father was accompanied by a young lady, whom his father introduced as Molly. His father explained, 'Molly works in the offices where I work, Samuel, and she is very interested in the bridges just like you. I told her we were going to see the Swing Bridge tonight, and she asked if she could come with us.'

When they reached the Swing Bridge, which had opened in 1876, Arthur reminded Samuel that he had told him the history of this bridge and it would have been good to see it in action but it was difficult to find out when it would be opening. One day they might be lucky.

'Yes, I remember you telling me about that bridge, Father, and I remember all that you told me about Sir William Armstrong. I also remember admiring that man and thinking how much I would like to be as successful as he was and also to be as clever an engineer as he was.

'Just tell me again, Father, how the bridge knows when to open because I think that is so clever.'

Samuel noticed that Molly never said a word and he could see that she was not interested. Why had his father wanted her to come? It did not make sense. She was still doing that silly giggling.

'Well,' said his father in answer to Samuel's question. 'As the ship approaches the bridge it sounds out three blasts on its steam whistle. The bridge answers with three blasts from its own siren and then using its hydraulic machinery swings open to allow the vessel through. We have to remember too, Samuel, that steam ships were now in use instead of sailing vessels and so loading on the Tyne was much brisker and allowed the ships to travel much more quickly to London where the coal was sent on to other countries.'

Samuel was so interested in what his father was saying that he had almost forgotten Molly's presence. He did not think girls would really be interested in bridges and ships but she did seem to be listening to his father, although she never asked any questions. He noticed, however, that every now and then she gave his father a little hug and seemed to be hanging onto his arm for a lot of the time. There was no need for that! She was in no danger of falling in the river. Nevertheless, his father seemed to like the hugs he was getting although he was sure his father would have liked his mother's hugs better. Molly kept giving little giggles when she caught his eye and he did not like it. Girls in his class were always giggling and he thought they were so silly. They giggled for no reason whatsoever as far as he could see. Grown-ups were funny sometimes!

Samuel had continued to meet his father after work until he was sixteen years old. He was by then of course attending the upper school at Todd's Nook which was not far from Snow Street. He was working hard, determined to do well and his ambition was, as in his younger years, to be an engineer. His father had managed to inspire him with all his information about famous North Eastern engineers. He wanted to go to university and one day as he was walking down to meet his father he had decided to bring that subject up with him. He was surprised, however, and disappointed, to see that he was not going to be alone with his father. That girl Molly, who looked so much younger than his father, was there again.

'Molly wants to walk back with us again, Samuel. She is going to walk up with us as far as St. Andrew's church.'

'Where do you live then?' Samuel asked politely.

'I live on Westgate Road, Samuel, so I go your way until we reach St. Andrew's church and then along Blandford Street to where I live.'

'Rather a long way round,' thought Samuel but it was not for him to question.

It was not the same that day. He loved having his father to himself and once Molly had left them, his father did not seem to want to talk much. In fact he said nothing all the way home. His mother even commented during their evening meal, saying, 'Arthur you are quiet tonight. Did you have a bad day at work?'

'No, pet, as good a day as I usually have, though there was a bit of trouble down the dock. Someone reckoned they were not being treated fairly but of course there is always somebody grumbling about that. What about you, pet, how was your day?'

'Well, alright, but I am a little bit worried about our Rachel. She is definitely not as strong as Esther and Samuel, Arthur. We went for a walk after school and had to come home because she said she was feeling very tired. She is only a young girl and should be full of energy. She also seems to pick up infections very readily and has missed a lot of school. I worry about her a lot.'

'Well she is getting tall so it is probably growing pains. Try not to worry too much.'

There was no mention of Molly, Samuel noted and something told him not to mention her at the tea table.

Life seemed to change from that day. Molly was always there when Samuel went to meet his father and his sisters were not much fun nowadays. They were young ladies now, they said, and did not want to play childish games. They used to love going to Leazes

Park with him when they would run around the lake and see who could do it in the fastest time and they also loved kicking a ball around but whenever he asked them to go with him they were not interested. He thought it might be because he insisted they held his hands when they were crossing busy Barrack Road, but it was for their own good. He was very protective of them. He thought they should have been grateful but they told their mother he was too bossy.

His mother was quiet these days and not as talkative as she used to be. He had no idea why and as for his father, he seemed to have much less to say than usual. His parents used to talk together about all sorts of things and often went for a walk in Leazes Park or down to the football ground and past the 'Strawberry Inn' where they sometimes had a drink before coming home. They never went out much together these days. Something was different. He was not the only one to feel things were a little different. Millie had noticed that Arthur never seemed to want to do anything or go anywhere with her. He seemed to be preoccupied but she had no idea why and when she challenged him about it he shrugged it off and said that he was getting older and just liked to spend time in his home.

One day about this time, Samuel asked if he could take his sisters to the quayside one Sunday morning because there were stalls and all sorts of things to amuse people, but his mother would not allow that. He was surprised then when his father said he would take all three of them, the girls and Samuel, to the quayside one Sunday morning. This was a surprise because their father usually liked to rest on Sundays, if he was not needed to help his mother with the washing. He could see that washing was hard work and his mother always had trouble with the poss stick. She was not very tall and pushing it down in the tub and then lifting it up and out of the hot tub of water was not easy for her. Monday was traditionally the washing day for everybody but Millie cheated by doing it on a Sunday, when Arthur could help her. Working on the Lord's Day was frowned upon, but many people did it, mainly for the same reason as Arthur and Millie.

However, Arthur had promised to take the girls to the quayside and he must fulfil his promise and the girls were so excited. The previous week of looking forward seemed to go so slowly but when at last Sunday came they got dressed up in their bonnets and best dresses and tried to walk sedately down the streets to the river. They had a lovely time and even met Molly down there. Father invited her to have a drink with them and she was so nice to him and the girls, although Samuel found himself wishing that it was just his father and sisters on this lovely day out. He also wished that his mother had come with them then it would have been the whole family, but she said she wanted to catch up on jobs, whatever they were. 'Why did Molly have to come?' he asked himself. The girls said she was so pretty but oddly their father told them not to talk about Molly when they got home.

'Why not?' said Esther. 'She's nice and Mother would like her.'

'Well we will bring Mother with us one day to meet Molly. Anyway, she is very busy just now with all her sewing for other people. She has promised to have some of it ready tomorrow, and is glad of the chance to get on with it. She will be anxious to know if Rachel has been alright because she does seem to be getting tired very easily.'

Sure enough, their mother fussed over Rachel when they got home and Molly was quite forgotten. Their mother wanted to know all about their trip to the quayside. Esther was bursting to tell her mother about the man who got tied up with so many chains and then had to get free from them. 'I never thought he could do it, Mother, but he did and everyone was clapping so hard. How did he do it, Father? Do you know?'

'Sorry, Esther. I am usually able to answer your questions as you know but to that one I have no answer.'

'Well we have had a lovely day, Father. Thank you! Can we go again?' She was just about to say that Molly might like to come with them again, when she remembered that her father had said their mother would not be interested in Molly.

'Of course we will go again and next time I hope your mother will come.'

After hearing all the chatter about their trip to the quayside, Millie promised that she would accompany them one day.

# Chapter 14

Samuel was still reminiscing when he remembered that he must take notice of this new bridge that had been built in his absence and it was a very important bridge for Newcastle. He got out of his seat and found a place where he could see the bridge clearly. Gosh it was spectacular. It had a huge arch and was a tremendous feat of engineering. His interest in engineering had never waned and he could not help wishing he had had a hand in the making of this iconic bridge. He had heard that at the time of its opening the previous year, in 1928, it was the largest single span bridge in Britain, spanning 531ft over the river. He had heard people say that it was built as a practice run for the Sydney Harbour Bridge in Australia, although it was nowhere near as big as the one in Australia. It was as far back as 1864 that the idea of a bridge over the river at this point was thought to be a good idea. There was a toll on the High Level Bridge which was not popular but it was 1924 before Newcastle and Gateshead authorities approved the construction of a new bridge over the Tyne. It would be iconic because it would let the traffic flow straight up Pilgrim Street and Northumberland Street and onto the North Road leading up to Scotland and beyond. It would open up to the higher parts of Newcastle and Northumberland Street would benefit greatly from this move away from the quayside. They would get much more trade. The new bridge would alleviate congestion on the quayside, where the streets were narrow, ill lit, and rubbish-strewn. In fact, the quayside, which had always been the centre of everything, was deteriorating rapidly. It became neglected and very dirty and unattractive while the new town centre, a good distance from the river, was flourishing.

Northumberland Street quickly developed into a very busy highway and shopping area, where businesses began to thrive. It had once consisted of private houses but the houses were gradually converting to business premises and large stores were being built.

The first of these was Fenwick's. It had been a doctor's house until it was bought in 1882 by a Mr John Fenwick, from Richmond in Yorkshire, who opened the premises as a small drapery shop. Over the years it developed into a large, successful, very popular Department store, one of the first in Newcastle. Another large store situated in the street was Marks and Spencer and so the street developed until it became a very important thoroughfare. Work started on the new Tyne Bridge in 1925 and the bridge was completed on February 28th 1928. Samuel wished he could have been in Newcastle when King George the fifth and Queen Mary opened the bridge on October 10th 1928. He had read about it in a London newspaper and it triggered something in him. He decided that he would go back to Newcastle very soon. He had already been away too long. Surely enough time had gone by now. No-one could possibly remember him.

Samuel was unaware at that point of a young lady travelling in the same carriage as himself, who was looking at him with a quizzical look on her face. Samuel had also caught the eye of a young man in the carriage but this recognition was not going to be good.

The train was nearing Newcastle now and soon it would be pulling into the station, the Central Station it was called, and what an iconic building it was. The train swept round in a curve before entering the station. Samuel opened the window slightly so that he could savour the pungent smell of steam, which was so special to steam engines and especially in a railway station, where the steam collected. It seemed to invade the nostrils and certainly it pervaded the railway stations. The train now crossed what became known as the Diamond Crossing, which had been constructed at the turn of the century and which at one time was the busiest and largest railway crossing in the world. As the train passed it Samuel noted the old Castle keep, which had been built in the 12th century near the River Tyne. It was in a remarkable state for its age and towering as it did over the river at the entrance to Newcastle it seemed to reach out with a welcome.

As the train shuddered to a halt inside the station Samuel had a tremendous feeling of being home. He could not help remembering the words embroidered in cross stitch across one of the pictures his grandmother had on one of her walls. It said 'There is no place like home'. How true those words were. He stood on the platform and savoured the smells and hustle and bustle and creaks and groans and hissings of steam engines, which were all part of a Railway Station.

There would be no-one to meet him because no-one knew he was coming, but that could not spoil the wonderful feeling within himself that he was back home. London was a great, big, exciting city, but it was not in his bones like Newcastle. What he was going to do or where he was going to go he had no idea, but he was home and at that moment in time, that was all that mattered.

Samuel marvelled at this great Central Station. He stood for several moments just savouring his surroundings. The Central Station was a lovely building. It was full of character and had been designed with great skill, his father had said. It was set in a large curve, because the land given for it to be built upon was rather restrictive, being small and curved. The main architect was John Dobson whose name was synonymous with many of Newcastle's great buildings. John Dobson was yet another very clever man emerging from Newcastle. Samuel had not been surprised to learn that that great engineer Robert Stephenson, to whom his father had often referred, was involved with John Dobson, on the construction of the Central Station. It was actually the last building John Dobson designed before he died in 1865.

Samuel's grandmother had told him that work had begun on the station in 1845 and that it had taken five years to construct. It had been opened by Queen Victoria and Prince Albert on August 29th 1850, nine years before his mother was born.

She also told her grandchildren about the visit of the King and Queen when they came to Newcastle to open the station. There was the usual banquet to celebrate the big occasion, in the Royal Station Hotel, which had been built next to the station. Unfortunately, and quite by accident, the queen was presented with the bill for the banquet by the Station Hotel manager. She took great offence, so much so that whenever her train carriage passed through Newcastle on her way to Scotland she drew down the blinds. What a story! Samuel never found out whether the story was true or not.

On his way out of the station Samuel stood and admired the portico of the station. John Dobson had intended the station to have a colonnaded front and an Italian style tower, but he never realised his vision. Later, however, in 1861 a portico which was designed by the architect Thomas Prosser, had been added to the station, making it even more imposing. Samuel loved the building and it was a good place to stand while he thought about what to do next.

# Chapter 15

It was some time before Samuel was aware that someone had come to stand beside him. It was a man about his own age and the man's first words were. 'Hi Samuel, remember me?'

'Sorry, I don't but who are you?'

'You do know me, Samuel. We were in the same rowing club and you were extremely good.' Samuel took a good look at the man, and realised that he did know him but had never had much to do with him. He could remember him being in the rowing club but he seemed to remember that he was often involved in the various altercations that occurred and was not very popular. In fact Samuel had an instinctive feeling that this man was trouble and he tried to move away. The man was Cuthbert Latimer, and he was not going to let Samuel go, as he had some business to do with him.

'Where are you living now?' he asked Samuel.

'Funny you should ask that,' was Samuel's reply, 'because I have just come back to Newcastle after living away for a number of years and my first priority is to find somewhere to sleep. I had better get going before it is too dark.'

'I am lucky, I suppose,' said Cuthbert, 'because I am going to stay with my sister. In fact I had better be on my way, because she will be wondering where I am. I am curious, though, as to why you left Newcastle and the rowing club so abruptly. Did it have something to do with that accident on the River Tyne after a

Rowing Regatta? It was quite a long time ago, about twenty years, I think.'

Samuel could not believe what he was hearing. No-one knew about that or at least he had always thought that. Surely the past was not going to catch up with him now after all this time? He had to think this through and get rid of this man.

'I have to go now,' Samuel said, 'but perhaps we can meet up sometime soon. Why not here outside the station in a week's time?'

'Great,' said Cuthbert, 'I will be there.'

Cuthbert could not believe his luck. A lucrative time could be ahead of him. He had much to ponder as he limped his way back to his sister's house in Elswick. This old war wound in his leg was becoming more and more painful. He would have to go and see about it. In fact, that had precipitated his return home because he wanted to see if the surgeon who had operated on his leg at the Royal Victoria Infirmary, a few years ago, could perhaps look at it again, and give him an idea as to why he was in such pain. It was definitely getting worse. It would make such a difference to him if something could be done to improve it.

Samuel too had much to ponder as he walked away from the station, but he must find somewhere to sleep for the night. He could not believe it! He had spent twenty years in London trying to forget 'the accident' that had changed his life and he was returning to his home town to finally put his past to rest and as soon as he stepped out of the station, the first thing to confront him was his past. It was unbelievable!

There were questions he wanted to ask Cuthbert. How did he know about the 'accident', and if he knew, how many other people knew? It was nearly enough to make him take a train back to London but not quite. He was curious to find out what this Cuthbert man had to say. Perhaps he should not have come back to the place where the 'accident' had taken place but in the end he decided that he would not make a hasty decision. He would find somewhere to stay and then really think about what he was going to do.

It would have been quite nice to stay at the Station Hotel, attached to the Central Station, an imposing Victorian Building. The hotel had been opened by Queen Victoria and Prince Albert, as a four star hotel, in 1858, though in 1890 a six storey extension was built and later a further two storeys were added. Samuel had heard that its rooms were sumptuously decorated but he certainly could not afford to stay there, even for one night. He would have to find somewhere else where he could do some serious thinking.

He was now jobless. He had left a good job in London and he would need a job in Newcastle. He had good qualifications, having studied at 'Armstrong College', which was named after the famous industrialist William George Armstrong, whom he had come to admire so much. Samuel wanted to study subjects that would assist him to be an engineer.

Newcastle had a School of Medicine and Surgery established in 1834 which was later called The College of Medicine, but there was a need for the teaching of Sciences in Newcastle and in 1871, a 'College of Physical Science' was founded which gave instruction in Mathematics, Chemistry, Physics and Geology. This College was later called Armstrong College, and it was this college which was attended by Samuel in 1900. It had been extended in 1888 and in 1894 and so was a sizable building when Samuel studied physics there. He worked hard and was awarded a degree in Physics in 1903. His parents were very proud of him. He had always been very special to them but it seemed he was even more special now.

He had been given an apprenticeship at the works of Charles Parsons in the east of the city. Charles Parsons was not a Tynesider, because he was born in Ireland, where he belonged to an aristocratic family and he was very well educated. When he came to England in 1877 he was well qualified but he wanted to learn more about water power and shipbuilding and armaments, and he wanted to learn it from the master himself, William Armstrong. He signed on as an apprentice at his factory in Elswick.

He was a clever man and actually became another famous man from Tyneside. This was largely due to his invention of a steam turbine which revolutionised ships' engines, naval warfare and the generation of electrical power and he designed and built an electrical generator. Later he designed and had built the steam turbine driven ship Turbinia and it was very much faster than any other ship of the time.

Samuel had been thrilled when he went to Charles Parsons's factory after his graduation. The factory had opened in 1889 for the manufacture of the turbine engine he had invented and which was adding so much to the industrial development of Newcastle. Samuel was thrilled to be furthering his ambition to be an engineer. Samuel was determined to make his mark on society but unfortunately his ambition was doomed by the 'accident' which changed his life for ever. In later years he often looked back to his graduation and how happy and proud his parents were of his achievement. He had a family photograph of his parents, himself and his sisters taken at that time and they were all smiling and happy. Who could have guessed then that their lives within a few years would be shattered and that happy family no longer existed.

Samuel had kept up his main leisure interest of rowing, during his college years and was very proficient at it. He loved competitions and was a popular leader of the sport in his rowing club. His father used to go with him to the rowing club and even learnt to row himself so he and Samuel spent some very happy hours together rowing on the River Tyne. There were always people who came down to the river to watch the rowing and one day Samuel saw a face he recognised. It was Molly, the young woman who used to accompany his father home from work. He had never liked her and somehow her presence disturbed him. Surely his father was not still seeing her, but it became clear that they were still good friends and

Samuel did not like it at all. He had thought that during the years he spent at Armstrong College, the friendship had ended.

He could not help wishing that his mother would come and watch his father and himself rowing. It might discourage Molly but Millie was not at all interested in the river, even though she had lived fairly near it all her life. Sewing had always been and always would be her hobby. Samuel knew that, but he could not help wishing that it was her and not Molly, who came to see them rowing. Inevitably on the fine days when Samuel and his father went rowing, his mother would take Esther and Rachel to the park or to the library. The girls always loved an outing to the park, even though Rachel still got tired easily and his mother worried about her so much.

Then in 1907 a dreadful thing happened. Rachel contracted diphtheria. Millie's meticulous nursing of her did not prevent her from being taken into hospital and to the family's great sorrow Rachel did not recover from the deadly disease. Arthur and Millie were devastated to lose one of their children, especially after she had been moved to the infectious diseases hospital and they had been given hope of her survival. Millie's sobs were heart-breaking and for quite a long time she was depressed and had to have medication. She blamed herself for Rachel's death. If only she had got the doctor sooner when Rachel had first felt unwell, her daughter might have survived. She was inconsolable.

It was a very sad, difficult time for the whole family. Samuel and Esther missed their sister terribly and to see their mother so unwell had a very sobering effect on them. When she was at her lowest point she asked Arthur if he could possibly take a little time off work to help her, but he did not want to do that. Millie knew then that their relationship was not as solid as it once had been. He would have done what she asked without hesitation at one time and not for the first time she wondered if there was a reason for his lack of consideration for her. He was so very quiet these days.

Rachel's death was a terrible blow for the family. Samuel tried to keep busy so that he did not have to think too much about what had happened. He was annoyed with his father because he seemed distracted and made no attempt to help his mother get over their loss, even though she asked him to try and get some time off work. His reply had been that he could not take time off as there was a backlog of work that must be done as soon as possible or there might be some redundancies.

One day Samuel got home from work a little sooner than usual and decided to go and meet his father from work just like he used to do and then he could perhaps have a talk with him and see what was making him so quiet and unco-operative. Their home was not the loving home it had once been. Something was wrong and he wanted to know what it was.

He walked to the quayside and along by the river to Armstrong's factory where his father worked. It was good timing because the men were just coming out of work. He recognised the man who came across to speak to him, as being one of the men his father worked with. 'Hello Samuel. How is your father? I hope he is getting better from his illness. We have missed him at work.'

Samuel was shocked but he managed to thank the man for his concern and say that his father would be back at work soon, before walking quickly back the way he had come. He could not believe his father's deceit. What was he thinking about? He should be with his mother helping her to get better. He started to run and sure enough when he reached St. Andrew's church he saw them, Molly and his father.

He ran up to them and shouted at his father. 'Father, you have not been going to work for weeks, so do not pretend that you have. Why are you deceiving Mother? Where have you been, as if I cannot guess?' Turning to Molly he said, 'Molly, my father is married to my mother and she needs him so much at this time when she is grieving for my sister. He should be with her and not you.' It was then that he saw with horror that Molly was heavily pregnant.

'Samuel, your father loves me not your mother and he is going to tell her so. I love him so much and I cannot live without him.'

Samuel was almost shouting at her. 'My father loves my mother Molly and you are just a silly girl. Father, I cannot believe what you are doing. Is the baby yours?'

'I am afraid so, son.'

'Have you taken leave of your senses, Father? What will mother say when you tell her because she will have to know – I will tell her if you don't.'

'Please, Samuel,' his father pleaded, 'do not do that until after the Rowing Regatta this Saturday. I know I have behaved abominably, but please, please, do not tell her yet. I am begging you, Samuel. I will tell her myself at the right time.'

'There is no right time, Father. You disgust me.' And Samuel ran away from them. He could not bring himself to go straight home in his present state and went to a friend's house until he cooled down. He would give his father until Saturday to tell his mother.

Arthur kept up the deceit until the Regatta Day. Millie, who was still grieving for her daughter, decided not to go to the regatta to see Arthur and Samuel take part. Arthur was going to assist Samuel in the same boat.

Esther said she would stay with her mother and she waved goodbye to her father and brother, not realising how much her life was going to change before she saw them again.

When they reached the river, Samuel was furious to see Molly there and rushing towards his father. It was even worse when his father held out his arms and caught her up in them, laughing and swinging her in the air. How dare he!

When it was time to board their boat, Molly stepped forward as if to climb aboard, but to Samuel's relief his father put out his arm to stop her. 'Not in your condition, Molly. We don't want anything to happen to you, do we?'

The race began, and Molly stood on the quayside waving at them but Samuel and his father concentrated hard on the race. It was very exciting and people were cheering and shouting to urge the contestants on. It was all rather frantic. Arthur and Samuel rowed very well indeed and were in third position when they reached the quayside again. Molly was waiting, still shouting and cheering and jumping up and down with excitement. It all happened so quickly after that that no-one fully realised what was happening. Molly went so overboard with her excitement that she actually fell overboard as it were, into the river, which of course was icy cold. Samuel immediately jumped in after her, gasping as the cold water hit his body but he then realised that Molly was hardly moving and making no sound. He was expecting his father to pull her aboard the boat and was all ready to help him, but his father seemed to have frozen on the spot because he made no attempt to help Molly. It was becoming obvious to Samuel that Molly's body had gone into shock with the coldness of the water and her pregnancy was not helping. She was very heavy, but he pushed her body up as near as he could to the top of the water and deck of the boat, shouting at his father to get hold of Molly and drag her into the boat. Still his father made no attempt to get hold of Molly. What was the matter with him? What he saw next was unbelievable. His father was actually pushing Molly's head down into the water while pretending that he was helping her. He was shouting, 'Come on, Molly, hang on to my hands and push, push, push.' Her body was going limp in Samuel's arms and he knew that she was drowning. His father was sitting staring ahead of him and not uttering a word. Samuel started to shout loudly for help but of course by the time help arrived it was too late to help Molly. She and the baby within her had died.

To any onlooker the incident would have looked like an accident. Arthur sat staring straight in front of him, obviously in a state of shock. He had been heard shouting to Molly to hold on and grasp his hands and no-one could have seen him pushing the head down under the water because he was facing away from the quayside as he ostensibly tried to save Molly. To all the onlookers, Arthur and Samuel had tried to save the young woman. The fact that she was pregnant had hampered their efforts to save her and she had died. No blame could be attached to anyone. In all the confusion of the crowds and the police arriving Arthur managed to disappear and make his way home.

Samuel stayed long enough to make a statement to the police that he had not witnessed the accident. He knew it was not the truth but he could not deal with the truth. He could not believe that his father had acted in the way he had. He had deliberately let Molly die. He had murdered her, because with Samuel's help he and his son could have saved Molly. Samuel was incredulous. How could his father do that? It was absolutely horrific. He felt sick and was sick and as he made his way home, he did not know how he could face his father again.

Molly should not have died. He even had guilty feelings because sometimes he had wished that something would happen to Molly, but never in his wildest dreams had he wished her dead. He just wanted her out of his father's life. A terrible thought came to him in the night. Had his father planned to somehow rid himself of Molly at the Regatta? After all, he had asked Samuel not to tell Millie until after the Regatta. Why had he stipulated that time? Surely, he would not deliberately plan to get rid of Molly? It was unthinkable.

Somehow the next few days and weeks passed, and all that Millie knew of the accident was the report she read in the newspaper, that a young pregnant girl had drowned on the day of the Rowing Regatta and that Arthur and Samuel had tried to save her. She had expressed her sympathy for the girl and her family but never found out the truth. She could see how shocked her husband and son were and she cared for them in her usual motherly way. She quickly realised, however, that the accident had affected her husband and son very much indeed. Samuel would not speak to his father and Arthur sat in his chair almost motionless every day. She thought it was all due to shock but the atmosphere in the house was unbearable. The doctor had to be called and Arthur was put on tablets after being diagnosed with depression.

There were no tablets of course that could ever help Samuel. He was full of hate for his father and could hardly bear to look at him. All he could think about was that his father was a murderer. He did not ever say to Samuel that he was sorry for what he had done. In the end Samuel could stand it no longer. He was so ashamed of his father and it was very hard not being honest with his mother. She did not deserve the shame his father had brought to the family if it became known that he had allowed someone to drown.

The strain of keeping his secret was very hard and his sister, Esther, was constantly telling him how different he was now. He used to be such fun but now he hardly spoke to his family, and especially not to his father. What was the matter with him? Life was just not easy at all and became increasingly difficult as they struggled to keep up the pretence that they were still in shock over the accident.

Millie was bewildered by the behaviour of her husband and son. It was now three months since the accident, but both her husband and son were finding it difficult to sleep and neither of them were ever hungry. She knew something must be wrong when she could not even tempt them to eat Nellie's special scones and pies. Her mother-in-law tried to help the family by visiting regularly and trying to talk to her son, because it frightened her to see him like that. It was worrying when he started to lose a lot of weight and was no longer interested in anything. Arthur was not sleeping and so dark circles appeared around his eyes. He had always been a handsome man but he looked dreadful now.

His mother had no idea, of course, of Arthur's torturous thoughts. What on earth had possessed him to betray his wife and family and how had he ever thought that killing Molly would answer his problems, because he had intended the accident to happen. He knew he had caused the destruction of two families and there was no reprieve for him. Besides, he could never forgive himself for what he had done. He saw the hate and suffering in Samuel's face every day and he was deeply ashamed of what he had done. There was no way out except to confess but that would mean prison and what would that do to his family? He just could not bear that.

Things were getting worse and in the end Samuel felt the only way forward for him was to leave home. He thought it best in everyone's interests to leave without telling anyone at all and so one night, through the night, he packed some clothing into a case, went down to the Central Station and took a train and his secret to London. He felt dreadful about leaving his job so abruptly and not telling his mother that he was leaving but he knew she would try to persuade him to stay. He was being very cowardly but he felt it had to be that way. He would write to Parsons when he got to London and try to explain to them the reason for his sudden departure and apologise profusely.

He would have to get a job when he got to London but his degree and his working experience at Parsons, would hopefully help him with that.

This proved to be the case and it was not too long before he got a job and saved just enough money to get settled into a hostel, while he tried to find a room to rent. It was very expensive to find any accommodation in London but he eventually managed to rent a room and was happy to work hard and keep himself occupied, so that thoughts of home did not dominate his life. In time he made friends and followed sport pursuits and managed to have a happy existence.

In order to make a new beginning in London he had reinvented himself. He had his dark shoulder-length curly black hair cut very short and he had grown a small beard which he cut regularly to keep it in shape though he allowed it to give him some sideburns, as he thought they looked distinguished. He had never bothered much about his appearance before going to London but even though he had a limited budget, he bought clothes in London which gave the impression of a smart city gent. He was proud of his appearance and often wondered what his mother and father and sister would have said about him now. He was sure they would approve because when he lived at home his mother was always telling him to smarten himself up, and she was always having to remind him to polish his shoes, which he hated doing. Well he now had some very smart 'brogues' which were the latest fashion. He really liked them and was sure his mother would have approved. He remembered his sister Rachel was constantly telling him, when he lived at home, that he should dress more smartly so she would have approved of his new look. He had pangs of guilt when he thought about Rachel because he had left his mother still grieving for his sister and he should have been there to help her.

He had pangs of guilt also about his sudden departure. He knew that he should have let Parsons know of his intention and he should have told his parents and given some sort of explanation for his departure to London, but he could not think of a way to tell them without including the accident and this would have involved telling the truth about his father, so he could not do it. He must keep the secret about his father, because the consequences of not doing so were too terrible to contemplate, but he really was ashamed of his behaviour.

Well, here he was returning to his beloved Newcastle, not at all sure what he was going to do.

There were bound to have been changes in Newcastle since his departure twenty years ago in 1909, at the age of 27.

There had been a war involving England and it had been very scary living in London. He remembered wishing he lived anywhere else but London at the height of the war. He felt himself very fortunate to have escaped being called up, because at a routine medical test he was found to have a heart murmur and so was exempt from service. He wondered why that had not been found sooner, but he had always been well growing up and the exertion of his favourite activity of rowing had never been a problem. He remembered how his mother had looked after her family so well and she would have worried terribly if she had known he had a heart defect. Well, it made no difference to him now. He carried on his life the same as always and he had survived the war and the years since, without any medication. It had never curtailed his life in any way. He was a survivor!

# Chapter 16

Now, standing outside the Station Hotel his immediate problem was finding somewhere to sleep. He walked past the hotel, making light of the fact that he carried quite a large suitcase, and made his way down to a building with which he was very familiar in his early twenties. He had inherited a great love for books when he was a small boy, from both his mother and his father. Even his grandfather had talked to him about his love of books, which was the reason for him being a member of the Literary and Philosophical Library and he talked a lot about the long hours he spent reading in the library. There were places in the library he had said which were made for you to sit comfortably and read your book.

Samuel remembered being able to read before he went to school. When he got to school he was the only one who could read in his class and he remembered that his teacher had sent him round the classes to read to each class and show them how clever he was. He certainly knew that you learnt things from books, which was why his father had been able to inform him about so many things while he was growing up.

His father's words came back to him. 'There is so much to learn about the world in which you live, Samuel, so always be inquisitive and ask questions and look things up in books.'

Books were just beginning to be more available when he was a teenager in the the late 1890s, and he thought it was a very good idea to be able to borrow books from a library as his mother did. Then came the day when he visited the special building which his father had told him about, in town. You could sit and read there to your heart's content, without any interference from anyone. That was what he needed at the moment, somewhere to sit alone and think, and so it was to this building that he now made his way.

The Library of the Literary and Philosophical Society was only a short walk from the station and once there he settled down to read and think about his next move. He had been reading for some time when a pleasant looking man, about the same age as himself, 47, came to sit near him. It was a place where conversation was allowed and so he and the man talked about their love of books and then the conversation moved on to other things. They exchanged information about themselves and Samuel divulged that he had just returned from London, after an absence of 20 years, and he would have to start looking for somewhere to stay. His newly acquired friend said that he was welcome to come back home with him until he sorted out his accommodation. He lived in Jesmond, a suburb of Newcastle, and was sure that his wife Catherine would not mind. They had three children who were in their teens, and their friends were always made very welcome in his home. His wife enjoyed company and anyone who came to their home was always made very welcome.

Samuel could hardly believe his good fortune and was extremely grateful to Isaac Boston, who preferred to be known as Dr Isaac. He told Samuel that he was a doctor working at one of the big hospitals in the city, namely The Royal Victoria Infirmary. Samuel told Isaac that he knew of the hospital because one of his two sisters had contracted diphtheria many years ago and had been in that hospital (when it was known as the Newcastle Infirmary) before she was moved to a special hospital for infectious diseases in Walkergate. There had been a fever hospital in Bath Lane since 1804 but it had become inadequate and that was when the new hospital at Walkergate was planned. Until it was ready a small wooden building was built in isolation on the Claremont Road side of the Town Moor. It was used as a fever hospital. until 1888 when the new hospital at Walkergate was opened. That small wooden building served its purpose admirably and stood empty, still in isolation, for many years after the transfer.

Samuel still shivered when he recalled that terrible time all these years later. His mother had been distraught and yet his father had done very little to comfort her. Samuel had known exactly why his father did not help her: he was too involved with Molly. Fortunately, his mother never knew that Molly was the reason for his father's disinterest and erratic behaviour and Samuel was determined she would never know.

Samuel liked Isaac and was so grateful for his offer of accommodation until he found somewhere more permanent to live and perhaps more importantly found a job. He had left a good job in London, but he still had to be careful with money and was conscious that he must contribute to his keep in Isaac's lovely home. Finally, he felt life was settling down again. Living with a family brought back memories of happier times in his life when he had been part of a family. He found Isaac's wife, Catherine, very pleasant and she never made him feel uncomfortable in any way. Indeed, she said that she enjoyed the extra company. Her husband was always so busy as a doctor in a busy hospital and sometimes they had very little time to talk, especially if he was on call and had to go into hospital through the night, to attend to a very poorly patient.

Samuel was a good listener and Catherine felt completely comfortable with him and enjoyed their conversations. He had shared with her his regret at not having found someone with whom he could share his life. He had had some good friends in London and enjoyed his life there, but he had never met or been drawn to any young lady with whom he could form a lasting relationship. He would have liked a family of his own, but obviously it was not to be. He did, however, so much enjoy spending time with Catherine and Isaac's children and was a very willing babysitter, because even though their children were teenagers their parents still liked an adult to be present if they went out socially. Catherine found a new freedom because she enjoyed the sport of badminton and rejoined the club to which she had belonged before her marriage. A doctor's wife could find her life quite restrictive as her husband worked very long hours and the main responsibility for their children would be hers. Throughout her children's childhood she had stayed at home to look after them and did not go out in the evening very much. She very much appreciated the help that Samuel gave her and they were good friends.

# Chapter 17

The children Edith, Edward and Thomas, really liked Samuel and they spent many happy hours together. He was very good company. He even surprised himself by enjoying a game of football in the large back garden. At the advanced age of 47 he had thought he was past such games but he had always loved sport and had kept himself fit, during his long stay in London. He often accompanied the boys to football matches at the Newcastle United Football ground in Gallowgate.

Another favourite activity he shared with Edith, Edward and Thomas, was long walks on the Town Moor and exploring Newcastle on foot. They often walked to the centre of Newcastle and decided which bit of it they were going to explore that day. Thomas, the eldest son, adored history and there was a great deal of history to be found in Newcastle. One day, Thomas decided that he wanted to know more about Grey's Monument. He asked Samuel many questions about this very tall landmark in the centre of the town. Samuel, who had made it his business over the years he was studying at Newcastle's Armstrong College to find out about some of Newcastle's iconic buildings, was well qualified to answer the questions he was asked.

They stopped beside Grey's monument and Samuel started by pointing out that there were 164 steps up the inside of the column and it was possible to arrange a viewing from the top of the monument, which is 133ft high. If anyone wanted to climb the spiral staircase, there were great views from the top and there was a proper viewing platform. Neither Edith, Thomas or Edward expressed a wish to climb the staircase, despite the promise of great views, but Thomas said that he wanted to know why it had been built, and the name of the man who stood on the top of it.

Samuel began to tell him as all the children seemed interested. 'The monument was built to honour the work of Charles Earl Grey who was born in Howick in Northumberland and was Prime Minister of England from 1830 to 1834. He was responsible for the passing of the Great Reform Bill of 1832 that gave the vote to businessmen, merchants and gentlemen farmers. Before this only the Freemen of the city could vote and that meant only 3,000 people out of a population of 53,613 in Newcastle could vote and if you would like to know more about the Freeman of our city, I can tell you later because my father told me all about them when I was a young lad and if you want to know I will tell you later.

'After the Reform Bill the number of voters rose to just short of 5000. Earl Grey also carried the act for the abolition of slavery in the colonies.'

'Well he is my hero,' Edward interrupted, 'because I hate hearing about how slaves were treated. We have been hearing about it in history lessons at school and the suffering of slaves is inhumane. Earl Grey deserves recognition for that.'

'Well,' Samuel continued, 'in 1836 he had a street named after him. It is the upper part of Dean Street which leads up from the River Tyne.'

'Grey Street is one of the finest streets in Newcastle, isn't it, Samuel?' Edith interrupted.

'It is indeed, Edith. You just need to stand at the top of Grey Street, near the Theatre Royal and look down the street to see the way it sweeps down in a curve towards the river and you will see why it is so impressive. Beautiful buildings can be seen on either side of the street as far as you can see.

'Two years later, in 1838, the monument was built at the top of Grey Street. It was Earl Grey's friends and admirers who were responsible for erecting the monument, by public subscription. It was to commemorate the 40 years the Earl had devoted to the cause of Parliamentary reform. Strangely enough, Earl Grey was never enthusiastic about the monument and did not seem to want the attention he was being given, but it went ahead. The sculptor, who was also responsible for Nelson's statue in Trafalgar Square in London, carved the twice life size statue of Earl Grey which sits on the top of the column and it was brought to Newcastle. It is difficult to understand why Earl Grey did not attend either the stone laying or the completion ceremonies.'

'I expect he found it all very strange having a memorial built to him when he was still alive,' Edith commented. 'But I think it was very kind of his friends to think about it and for the public to contribute to its cost. I hope Earl Grey did thank them for their efforts eventually.'

'One more thing to say,' Samuel continued, 'is that the monument first stood on an island, around which traffic circled, which made it quite dangerous. As you can see it has more paving around it and is not now so dangerous.

'Now is there anything else this morning that you want to know about before we go and get some lunch?'

'Yes there is,' Edward said quietly, because he was a quiet person, who never had a lot to say although he was a clever young man. 'I like the building opposite the monument which is an unusual shape. It is triangular and it is really on three streets, Grey Street, Grainger Street, and Market Street and on each of the three corners of the building there is a dome.'

'I am glad you have asked that, Edward, because it has a history and is a very fine building, but it has gone through some bad times.

'It was first known as 'The Central Exchange' built by Richard Grainger in 1837, when this man was developing the city with his brilliant designs for buildings. It was a commercial trading centre and a newspaper reading facility and was opened, apparently to great acclaim, in June 1839. To gain membership of the Exchange a guinea was charged and it was a privilege to be a member.

'Unfortunately the building has had two destructive fires. One was in 1867 and the other in 1901, and it has been closed for restoration several times. Membership declined and in 1870 the building relaunched itself as an Art Gallery. Then in 1891 the interior was remodelled to provide further rooms in an attempt to create a centre for social and cultural activities, such as smoke and chess room, billiard room, art gallery, meeting room, gentlemen and ladies' reading rooms, refreshment area and even photography and art clubs. A concert hall was even built within it in 1893 but the second fire in 1901 destroyed the interior of the building and it was decided to transfer the Art Gallery to The Laing Art Gallery, next to the Central Library, which was purpose built as a home for fine arts.

'It needed a massive refurbishment after the fire of 1901 but reopened in 1906 and became 'The Central Arcade' and that is what it is called to this day. Shall we go and look inside the arcade now? Because you have to see its beautiful interior. The architecture is wonderful and you must be sure to look upwards to appreciate the wonderful ceiling of inlaid wood. I also want you to take note of the beautiful shiny tiles of yellow and brown on the walls and then look down at the paving of vitreous mosaics, upon which you are walking. I think the whole building is unique and I hope it will always be looked after and kept in such a good condition.'

'We have had a very interesting day, Samuel and learnt so much. Thank you,' said Edward, and Edith and Thomas agreed with him.

# Chapter 18

One evening when Isaac and Samuel were sitting relaxing after their meal, the subject of Education came under discussion. Samuel told Isaac about the school he had attended which of course was Snow Street School and how he had enjoyed his time there. He had been fortunate enough to be able to attend Armstrong College, to study for a degree in Physics and he recalled again the pride on his parents' faces as he was awarded his degree. He stressed to Isaac that his parents were fine people and he had loved them both and his siblings very much indeed, which made Isaac wonder all the more why Samuel did not seem to contact them now, and why he had gone to London, all that time ago and for so long. If he was so happy living at home as he had indicated why did he not talk much about his parents or siblings? Where were they now? Surely, he would have sought them out now that he was back in Newcastle? Isaac tried to broach the subject with his new friend, but it was obvious that he did not want to talk about it. Perhaps when they knew one another better Samuel would open up to him.

Meanwhile, Samuel seemed to want to know more about Isaac. 'Well, first of all, Samuel, I have been fortunate in my upbringing. My parents had lived their young lives in the suburb of Jesmond, which was generally thought to be one of the richest places to live. We lived in a large house and my mother was able to have help to look after our family. I had two brothers and two sisters, and we attended a school called West Jesmond until we were 12 years old. Then I was sent to be educated at the Royal Grammar School, which was and still is, in my opinion the best boys' school in Newcastle

'The school was founded as long ago as 1544 when Thomas Horsley, a Mayor and one of the richest merchants in Newcastle, left money in his will for the founding of the Newcastle Royal Grammar School. It moved six times until in 1906 when it came to its Jesmond home and where it remains to this day. Initially the school was built to accommodate about 500 boys but the number has steadily increased over the years. Both of my brothers attended that school and my sisters attended the Central High School, which is almost directly opposite the Royal Grammar School. My wife went to that school, but I did not meet her during our school days. I met her at the church which my parents attended. You will have seen the church I am talking about, Samuel, when your train came across the Tyne Bridge. It has a very tall spire and is very near the Tyne Bridge.'

'Oh yes, Isaac, I know the church you mean. It looks different from other churches because of its oval shape, but that is quite a long way from Jesmond and Gosforth, isn't it?'

'Yes, but my father, like you, Samuel, from what you have told me, had a fascination for the Bridges over the River Tyne and when we came out of church he always took us for a walk along the quayside so that he could point out all the bridges and he always gave us details of their history, which we came to know off by heart.'

'Well, Isaac, my father taught me so much about the bridges when I was quite young because he loved the river and its bridges, so that is something we have in common and that church you are talking about certainly has a very tall tower and spire. I can see that it is different from other churches because of its oval shape.'

'Yes,' replied Isaac, 'and it is one of only four in the country. I once heard it described as one of the treasures of Newcastle. It is supposed to be one of the finest Georgian buildings in the country, so I am quite proud that my family went to that church.'

'Has it always been there, Isaac?'

'No, but there has been a church on that site since the 13th century. It was called 'All Hallows' then but that church had to be demolished in the 18th century and in 1786, architects were asked to submit designs for a new church. A man called David Stephenson put in a rather unique design which was accepted and in 1789 most of the church was complete and it was consecrated by the Lord Bishop of Durham. David Stephenson revised the design of the tower, which was completed in 1796. The sad thing is, Samuel, that the congregation is decreasing rapidly now because so much business has moved away from the river and quayside and my parents think it will not be long before the church has to close. It is such a pity and will feel strange if we have to move to another church.'

'My parents were church people, Isaac,' Samuel now said. 'They told me about their wedding in St. Andrew's church, which is the oldest church in Newcastle, and we used to pass it regularly when we walked into the town centre. It dates right back to the 13th century and there is so much history about it. It even has a leper's peephole in the outward wall from which the lepers could follow the service because they were not allowed in the church. I do not think many churches have one of those and I did hear that some 'witches' were buried beside the churchyard wall, when their bodies were taken down from the gallows – not that I believe in witches, I hasten to add. My mother told us that my two sisters and I were all baptised in St. Andrew's church but we have never attended church regularly. Perhaps I would have been a better person if I had made church part of my life. I will never know that for certain. What I do know, Isaac, is that I am so glad that I found you and that I am benefiting from your kindness. I must think through now what I am going to do about my future, so I will be off to bed'

'Goodnight Samuel. Sleep well.'

Samuel did not sleep well that evening. There was too much to think about. He lay awake going over everything that had happened. He knew that time was passing, and he could not be reliant on Isaac for too long. He had to move on and make a new life for himself. He was greatly enjoying the company of Isaac's teenage children and he almost allowed himself to be happy again, but he was worried about the man called Cuthbert whom he had met outside the station.

# Chapter 19

He had gone to meet the man as he had promised one week after their first meeting and they had found somewhere locally to eat and talk. Samuel's unease was awakened immediately when Cuthbert said he wanted to talk about the accident at the Rowing Regatta, 20 years ago.

'Why do you want to talk about that?' Samuel asked.

'Because I know what really happened,' Cuthbert replied.

'What do you mean by that?' Samuel said. 'It was a dreadful accident.'

'Well that is just it,' Cuthbert continued. 'It wasn't an accident, because I saw what happened. You see, Molly, who died, was a friend of my sister and as soon as she spotted Molly on the quayside she waved at her to get her attention. The boats were coming to shore after the race and Molly was jumping up and down with excitement when she saw my sister waving at her. She half turned to acknowledge my sister while continuing to wave and jump up and down and it was then that she lost her balance completely and plunged into the icy water of the river. You, Samuel, jumped in after her but it was obvious you were having difficulty lifting Molly up into the boat. There was a man in the boat, Samuel and that man was your father, as you know. My sister had by this time run down to the quayside and she actually saw what was happening. Instead of helping Molly, your father was pushing her head down under the water, every time you pushed her up for your father to grab.

It was only because she was so close that my sister saw what was happening. There were so many people milling around but not one was really aware of your father's deadly deed because he had his back to the shore. No-one could see what he was doing with his hands and arms. Your father got away with it, Samuel, and it was murder. When the police eventually came, they questioned a lot of people, but no one came forward with any information, so they had no proof of any wrongdoing. My silly sister did not speak up because she was still in shock, I suppose. There was an investigation, but the conclusion was that it had been a dreadful accident. You and I know it was not an accident, don't we, Samuel and I think I will tell the police what really happened.'

'No-one would believe you after 20 years,' Samuel said with bravado, although inwardly he was terrified.

'Well I could try,' said Cuthbert. 'I might start by looking up Molly's sister Prudence. My sister will know where she lives because of her knowing Molly. They both lived with their mother. Yes, I will pay her a visit and see where I go from there. Actually, I have just remembered that your mother does not live far away from my sister's house, in Stanhope Street. Nice woman. I wonder what she would say if I told her the story?'

Samuel was really worried now. He had kept the secret all these years and his mother must not find out now.

'Look, Cuthbert,' he said hurriedly, 'what would it take for you never to tell your story to anyone?'

'Well, I must think about it,' was the reply. 'We will have to meet again two weeks from now, same time same place.'

'Agreed,' said Samuel, relief showing in his voice, as he stood up to go.

'See you soon then,' he said as he walked away.

Samuel felt so dreadful that he decided to have a walk along the quayside, to try and clear his mind of his gloomy thoughts. He walked a long way, and did not notice that he was walking away from the river up towards Byker and Heaton. It was not too far from there to get to Parsons Engineering Works in Heaton where he used to work and he made a quick decision to go into the office where he asked if there was any work available. He had to be honest and he told them that he had worked there, twenty years ago. To his great surprise he was told to come back for an interview at a given date and as a result of that he was given a job. He was delighted and returned to Isaac's home in very high spirits that day. This did not, of course, solve the 'Cuthbert' problem but at least he would be earning money again, and it could be that in the near future he was going to need it.

His new job was to begin in a few weeks' time. Up to then Isaac had been taking Samuel into the hospital with him. There was always maintenance work at the hospital, on the numerous and often complicated pieces of equipment, and Samuel, with his engineering skills, was very useful to have around the hospital. He made himself invaluable and also earned some money while doing this, most of which he gave Isaac for his keep. The work had helped to take his mind off his next meeting with Cuthbert, as of course did all the time he spent with Isaac's family.

# Chapter 20

Samuel enjoyed working at the hospital. It was an impressive building, with an impressive entrance. The stature of Queen Victoria, mounted on a white pedestal, immediately drew attention to the fact that the hospital was named after her being called 'the Royal Victoria Infirmary' or RVI for short. The hospital had been built to commemorate the year of the Queen's Jubilee. The building of it began in 1900 and was completed in 1906. Sadly the Queen never saw its completion, having died in 1901. The hospital had begun life in 1751, situated behind the Central Station in Forth Street, but in 1897 a decision was made to make the hospital more central and land was given from the Corporation and Freemen of the city, on the Castle Leazes Moor, which had once been part of the Town Moor. King Edward VII opened the hospital on July 11th 1906. It was a very busy hospital and had a great tradition of caring. Isaac explained that this was particularly true during the First World War, when three extra pavilions were constructed temporarily nearby, to care for the injured. Samuel was very impressed with what Isaac told him. He could not help thinking of his own life and what he had achieved. It was not much, after all, but there was one thing which he thought he had got right. He had not betrayed his father and had no intention of ever doing so.

At his second meeting with Cuthbert the latter said that he had had made up his mind to go to the police with his story unless Samuel gave him a specified amount of money. Samuel was horrified. What was he going to do? This was a horrific situation for Samuel. There was no-one he could turn to for advice. He felt the only answer was to do what Cuthbert wanted, although he knew in principle it was not the right thing to do. He did not want to be involved in the whole sordid business but at the same time he did not want to be questioned by the police.

This new beginning, which he was enjoying so much, was being threatened by Cuthbert. He told Cuthbert that he would need a little time to get the money together, and a meeting in four weeks' time was arranged. He did note, however, that Cuthbert was not so sure of himself as he had been on previous occasions. He had appeared so smug and confident but now he seemed edgy and nervous and much more subdued. In fact, he found himself asking Cuthbert if he was well because he looked very tired and weary.

'I am fine,' Cuthbert told him, 'apart from my leg. It is really painful, but I am tough. I do not let anything, or anyone, get the better of me. See you in four weeks and you had better have the money.'

It was a sobering thought for Samuel that this episode in his life was very badly timed. He was going to need money himself to buy somewhere to live. He could not go on living with Isaac for an indefinite period. He would have to find somewhere to live and he would then need money to furnish his premises.

Meanwhile, in Jesmond, Isaac had noticed that his new friend seemed preoccupied but when he mentioned it Samuel said he was looking for a house and starting a new job and he couldn't help worrying about it. In order to try and cheer him up Isaac told him that he had invited a young lady to a meal at their house. She was a nurse at the RVI and quite often she worked on the same ward as himself. One day in conversation she had told him about her school days at Snow Street School.

He remembered that Samuel had told him that he had attended that school and thought it would be nice for them to meet up. The nurse was called Prudence. The evening of the meal was a great success. There seemed to be an instant attraction between the two young people and the conversation flowed effortlessly. The evening ended with Samuel asking Prudence to meet him in Newcastle the next evening, and Samuel felt better than he had done for a long time. He also slept better that night because his mind was filled with thoughts of Prudence and was not dominated by Cuthbert.

He had managed to draw enough money from his account in time for his next meeting with Cuthbert but again he could not help thinking about the inconvenience of the situation. He was at a time of his life when he was going to need a lot of money himself, especially if his friendship with his new friend Prudence developed into a steady relationship. He would need money to make a future with her. He certainly found her attractive and enjoyed her company.

He approached the meeting place at the Central Station for the fourth time with a heavy heart but to his surprise Cuthbert was not there. Instead a lady about his own age stood there. She spoke very politely to Samuel, asking him if he was waiting for someone named 'Cuthbert'.

'I am his sister Clara and he has asked me to come and speak to you.'

'You have the right person, Clara. I am Samuel.'

'Well I have come in my brother's place to tell you that my brother is in hospital and is unable to meet you today. I have been looking after him for several weeks. He has never quite recovered from the war, you know, because he sustained a very nasty injury to his leg. It was not treated well and keeps developing an infection. The pain he has been having has been very intense and so he has been taken into hospital. He has told me to ask you to meet him again here in four weeks, by which time he will be feeling much better. He also said that you might have something to give me for him. He also wants you to know that he has found out where your mother lives and will be going to see her very soon. I do not know what that is all about but no doubt you do.'

Samuel had to think quickly as a feeling of panic rose within him. He had to stop Cuthbert, in some way, from going to see his mother. He did, however, not want to give money to Cuthbert's sister.

'I need to think about this,' he said. 'I would much rather give it to Cuthbert myself. Could I meet you again in a few weeks' time when Cuthbert is able to come himself?'

'Well I am not sure what Cuthbert will say but I will agree to that,' Clara replied.

During the course of those four weeks Samuel took Prudence on several dates, all of which helped him to forget the 'Cuthbert' problem. Prudence had told him that she liked walking and he suggested that they had a walk on the Town Moor where they could visit the Exhibition Park. Samuel met her out of work one evening outside the RVI where she worked and from there it was a short walk into the park. The lovely Exhibition Park, which opened in 1887, was known as the Town Moor Recreational Ground, and was 35 acres in size. It was this section of the Town Moor which was used to hold 'A Royal Jubilee Exhibition' in 1887 to celebrate the fiftieth anniversary of Queen Victoria's reign. It was later given the name 'The Exhibition Park' in 1929 when the North East Coast Exhibition was opened by HRH the Prince of Wales. The exhibition was an attempt to raise people's spirits, in the aftermath of the First World War which had badly affected local industry and commerce, and people were struggling with all sorts of problems. There were many people hungry and homeless. The exhibition lasted six months and was very successful, having been attended by more than 4.3 million visitors.

Samuel and Prudence visited the park regularly when they were first going out together in1932, and really enjoyed the time they spent there. Sometimes a brass band was playing in the bandstand

and they would stop and listen. One other nice feature of the park was at the boating pool. A replica of the 1929, North East Exhibition had been built on the top of the existing bridge over the small lake and it was most effective in enhancing the boating pool. Samuel and Prudence quite often took a boat out on the pool and got a really good look at the clever construction of the exhibition on top of the bridge.

During all the time they spent together Prudence knew nothing about Samuel's meetings with Cuthbert. He just could not bring himself to tell her. He did not want to spoil his newfound happiness. However, the fifth meeting with Cuthbert did not happen. This was the second time Cuthbert had missed a meeting but his sister Clara had come again and she explained that Cuthbert was very poorly. The infection in his leg had taken a serious turn and there was danger of septicaemia or blood poisoning setting in. The doctors were very worried about him, but he was hopeful of getting better and being able to meet up with him again in a few weeks' time. A date was arranged but as before Samuel did not hand over any money. On the arranged date it was Clara again who met Samuel and she was very tearful. Her brother Cuthbert had sadly died of septicaemia. Whilst being very sympathetic Samuel could hardly contain his relief. His secret was safe! He never handed over the money for Cuthbert to Clara but he did give her some money towards Cuthbert's funeral for which she was very grateful and Samuel was equally grateful that she never asked him any awkward questions.

# Chapter 21

With the threat of Cuthbert over, Samuel felt much more relaxed about his friendship with Prudence and loved spending time with her. They talked at length about their circumstances and Prudence felt entirely comfortable sharing the fears and anxieties she had experienced in her life.

One day, Prudence told Samuel about seeing him on the train, a few months prior, when she was coming back from staying with her sister in London, in 1929. She had recognised him as being a pupil at Snow Street School and on reaching Newcastle she had decided to make herself known to him. She had come out of the station and saw him standing looking around him as if uncertain of what to do next and just as she was going to walk forward to speak to him, a middle aged man had moved over to speak to him. At that point she had given up, and taken the tram home to her little house on Stanhope Street where she lived alone. She was on duty at the hospital the next day and needed a good sleep. She did not tell Samuel that she slept very badly that night because she kept thinking about him and wishing she had spoken to him.

She could hardly believe her good fortune that she was now dating him. He was so good looking. She would be the envy of all her friends if they knew she was dating the best-looking boy in their form, when they attended Snow Street School. A number of girls in the class had had a crush on him. He was very brainy too and was always reading because he loved books so much. She seemed to remember that he had been the only boy who could read when he started school.

Samuel had got a very nice surprise when he met Prudence. She was pretty and well dressed and they had liked one another from the start. She was interesting, and he enjoyed spending time with her. On one of their outings Samuel suggested that he could call her Prue and he was surprised at her reaction. She said that she liked to be called by her full name, Prudence because that was the name her parents had given her, and she did not like it shortened. To her surprise Samuel started laughing. 'I know exactly what you mean, Prudence because like you I do not like my name shortened. I will not answer to Sam. I insist on Samuel. Isn't that a coincidence and another thing which we have in common? It is interesting that you recognised me on the train, although I have to be honest and say that I did not recognise you, as being someone I had known at Snow Street. I am, however, very glad to have met you now. Tell me a little about yourself.'

She told him that she lived alone now. She had had two sisters but one of them had died in a tragic accident on the River Tyne, and her other sister lived in London. Her mother had never got over losing one of her daughters and had died within a year of the accident. Prudence had had to leave her job in a local shop to look after her mother who was so distraught that she made herself an invalid for the rest of her life. She was very demanding and would not allow visitors or have anything to do with the outside world. She went over and over the story of her daughter's death in the River Tyne until Prudence felt like screaming. She did feel sorry for her though and it was very sad seeing her mother's health deteriorating. She had once been a very active person, very involved in church activities and always ready to help anybody in need. She seemed tothink she was in some way to blame for her daughter's death, because she should have gone with her that day and been more protective of her.

'Well I think she was very fortunate to have a daughter like you to look after her,' Samuel commented, 'and she ought to have been very thankful.'

'Well perhaps she was,' said Prudence, 'but we will never know now. I had no social life at all and never thought I would ever have a boyfriend but when she died I missed her dreadfully.

'I was, however, determined to make something of myself as I did not want to work in a shop for the rest of my life. I had always wanted to be a nurse and so I decided to train to be a nurse. It is the best thing I have ever done.

'I did my training at the Royal Victoria Infirmary and was lucky enough to get a job there when I finished my training. Did you know, Samuel, that the old workhouse site on the West Road is going to be made into a hospital? I have heard it is going to be called 'The General Hospital' – perhaps I will work there one day but meanwhile I am very happy at the RVI.'

'Please tell me a little more about the workhouse, Prudence, because I do remember that large building on the West Road, but I did not know anything about it.'

'Well it was called the 'Union Workhouse' originally and opened in 1839 to care for 'the able-bodied poor', 'imbeciles', 'pregnant women' and 'the sick'. It was extended in 1869 when a school room was built behind it and a bake house, a laundry and workshops. I once walked right round the workhouse on one of my lunchtime walks and I found some names which had been carved into the stonework, in its early days. One was 'the bake house' and another 'the sewing room'. I wonder what they looked like when they were part of the workhouse. The workhouse also took in tramps who were given a bath, bed and breakfast, and some sort of job to do in the workhouse before they were free to go on their way.

'In 1870 a hospital called the 'Poor Law Infirmary' was built and was later known as the 'Union Infirmary' In 1920 it changed its name again to the 'Wingrove Hospital'"because Wingrove Road ran down one side of the building. Then in 1930, Samuel, not too long ago, 'The City Council Health Committee' took over the hospital naming it the 'Newcastle General Hospital'. I wonder if Dr Isaac will ever work there, although I would hate him to leave the RVI because he is such a nice man and I have him to thank for meeting you. If he had not asked me for dinner that night we might never have met again, and I am so enjoying going out with you.'

'Well the feeling is mutual,' Samuel said. 'Do you still live in the house you were brought up in?'

'Oh yes, my mother left it to me. I get lonely in it sometimes, but I have a lot of nice friends and am not lonely for long. I am talking and talking, Samuel. Have you got any more to tell me about your family?

# Chapter 22

Prudence had noticed that Samuel did not have a lot to say about his home and family and he never talked about London and his reason for moving there, but it did not bother her too much. She was just happy that he wanted to spend time with her because she certainly enjoyed being with him and having someone in her life who was such good company and such a good friend.

As the weeks turned into months they each knew they were falling in love. One evening they discussed their future together and Prudence insisted that Samuel should tell her more about himself. She had given him a lot of detail about her life and it was his turn now, but he urged her to finish telling him about her life. He wanted to hear about the sister who had died in an accident, and he promised that he would talk about himself when she had told him about that. He did not quite know why, but he felt uneasy about the sister who had died in an accident on the River Tyne.

Prudence began by telling him that her younger sister, Molly, had always been a bit of a problem. Her parents had worried a lot about her because she was so different from her elder sisters. She was not as intelligent and very immature for her age. She was often in trouble at school and her parents were called into the primary school many times about her lack of progress and her behaviour. She was no better when she went to secondary school. In fact, it was worse. She was not interested in school work and kept company with the badly behaved trouble makers in the school. Her parents were actually relieved when she left school at 15, although that presented the problem of how she was going to earn money and become more independent. It was obvious she had very little academic ability but a friend of their father managed to get her a cleaning job at Armstrong's Factory in Elswick. 'My parents were so pleased, as she seemed to settle down well but they were not happy when she came in and said she had a boyfriend. My father asked her who he was, but she would not tell him, so he went down to the works one day to try and find out and saw her with a much older man. He was furious and even more concerned and furious when he found out that the man was married. Both my father and mother tried talking to Molly but of course it was useless. She would not listen and refused to give up her boyfriend. This went on for some time until my father took ill very suddenly with a heart attack and sadly died. It was a nasty shock for the family and Molly took it very badly, crying all the time. She stayed in bed most days and refused to come out of her room. She was very rude to my mother and shouted at my other sister and me all the time. She was very difficult to deal with and the only bit of consolation was that she was not seeing her boyfriend any more. We of course never brought up the subject and hoped that that was the end of the relationship. It took time but Molly did seem to be coping better and dealing with her became much easier.She even went back to her old job as a cleaner in the Armstrong Factory and life became normal again. Unfortunately the period of calm did not last...

'Molly seemed much happier and was always keen to get to her work in the early morning and late evening. Eventually Molly told my mother that she was seeing her boyfriend again. One morning my mother heard Molly being very sick and a visit to the doctors with her confirmed her worst fears: Molly was pregnant.

'We were all worried because Molly was so childlike herself and certainly not mature enough to look after a baby. She was only 17 years of age, much too young to have the responsibility of a tiny new life. It was suggested to Molly that she have a termination but she screamed and screamed at the top of her voice and it took ages to calm her down. My mother decided that she would have to take full responsibility of the baby when it was born despite anything Molly and her boyfriend said, though she did not tell Molly that of course.The pregnancy progressed, and Molly seemed to walk around in a trance, dreaming of the baby and her future with her boyfriend. She told us that her boyfriend had promised to leave his wife when the baby was born and he would buy a house for them to live in happily ever after. The atmosphere in our house was tense and terrible but we could do nothing about it. Molly went on and on about the lovely baby she was going to have and how she would dress it and play with it. It would be the best baby in the world. She was living in a fantasy world.

'Then came the day of the Rowing Regatta. Molly said she was going to it with her boyfriend, but neither Mother nor I went with her. I was working at the corner shop at the time and that was where I got the news that my mother needed me desperately. I got home as quickly as I could, to find a policeman with my mother. There had been an accident at the Rowing Regatta and he wanted me to go down to the quayside and identify the body of the young pregnant girl whom they had been told was my sister. She had drowned in the River Tyne. It was the worst experience of my life, identifying my sister.'

It was at this point that Prudence noticed that Samuel had lost all his colour and looked as if he was going to faint. 'Samuel, are you alright?' she asked him. Samuel definitely was not alright. He had been listening to Prudence with horror and there was no doubt in his mind that his father was the father of Molly's baby and that he was responsible for her death. Memories of that horrific day came flooding back. The dreadful truth was that his father had murdered Samuel's girlfriend's sister. It was unbelievable. What was he going to do now? How could he possibly marry Prudence knowing that his father had killed her sister? He just could not do it but he could not bear the thought of losing Prudence. He had been on the point of proposing to her. He had such plans for their life together. There was no need for a long engagement because they were both in their late forties now and must make the most of their time together, but it was not to be.

Samuel's world was shattered yet again and there followed a very difficult, unhappy time for both Samuel and Prudence. The latter was shattered that Samuel no longer wanted a relationship with her and could not understand or think of any reason why Samuel would not want to continue their relationship. Samuel could not possibly tell her the real reason for their break-up and he felt absolutely dreadful about it. Prudence cried and cried about it when she was alone, in her house, because she had been sure that Samuel had loved her as much as she loved him. Somehow, she had to build her life again and she concentrated on her nursing, doing as many shifts as she could possibly fit in at the hospital. She tried to avoid Dr Isaac because her eyes were always red, and he would be sure to want to ask about her friendship with Samuel because he was very interested in both of them. She could not have trusted herself to talk about him without getting very upset.

She was not aware then that Dr Isaac was also going through a very difficult time, although she had noticed when she did see him around the hospital that he was not his usual congenial self.

Some time later she heard from another nurse that his wife was very ill indeed. She was dying from cancer. Catherine was such a lovely lady and it was tragic for her family. Prudence could not help thinking about Samuel and how upset he would be because he had told her that he had lived with the family when he first returned to Newcastle, after 20 years' living in London, and Catherine had been very kind to him. Somehow it helped Prudence thinking about Samuel and Dr Isaac's family because it took her mind off her own troubles, and she was extremely sorry to hear the news that

Catherine had died. Many people attended her funeral, including Samuel and Prudence who both avoided looking at one another and made no attempt to talk to one another after the funeral at Dr Isaac's house. They made their escapes fairly quickly. Prudence, however, continued to visit the family and help in any practical way she could to alleviate their sorrow. Dr Isaac was finding it very difficult to cope with his busy life as a doctor and looking after his three children, who needed so much support. Edith, Edward and Thomas were still young people, unused to death and felt a great sense of loss.

Dr Isaac was extremely grateful for all the help Prudence gave him. She was happy to do housework chores and cook meals for the family and she certainly helped to keep the family together during that dreadful time. He did not know what he would have done without her. Life was sometimes very hard for Prudence because Samuel was a frequent visitor to Dr Isaac's home and there was still an awkwardness between them. Gradually, however, they became more comfortable with each other and the unbearable hurt began to ease. They found the company of Edith, Edward and Thomas to be a healing process because they were both so in earnest about helping the family and their own feelings took second place to that. Prudence reflected that had Samuel been her main concern when Catherine died she might not have been able to give so much time to Isaac and his family. She was also so glad to have found a new friend because she and Edith became very close. Edith felt the loss of her mother very keenly and she found Prudence a very good listener when she needed to talk about her mother. She was able to pour out all her grief and heartbreak to Prudence and it was such a comfort.

Edith was a very pretty girl, who looked very like her mother. Her long fair hair had a natural wave in it and looked so pretty hanging down to her shoulders, and she always looked fashionable because she made her own clothes and was very conscious of fashion. Her ambition was to be a fashion designer, and her sewing machine was well used as she experimented in making garments she had designed. She used to get cross with her brothers because in her opinion they were never smart. They liked to dress casually. They were very keen on sport and often accompanied Samuel when he went to the rowing club where he was a member.

Before Prudence became involved with Dr Isaac's family, after she and Samuel parted, she had considered leaving Newcastle, to live nearer her sister and her two nephews in London but she was now very glad that she hadn't left because those days looking after Dr Isaac and his family were, she realised, some of the happiest of her life. Nothing and no-one could ever replace Samuel in her heart but life took on some meaning for her again. She had also started to go to church again at St. Phillip's church, near where she lived. The minister welcomed her warmly into the family of the church and she was making friends there. It also gave her the opportunity to pray for Dr Isaac's family.

# Chapter 23

Some months later a new patient arrived on the ward where Prudence worked and while admitting her to the ward, which involved getting certain personal details, Prudence realised that the lady lived very near her, in Douglas Terrace. It was only a short walk from there to Stanhope Street, where Prudence lived, but she had never met the lady, prior to her admission to hospital. She was a woman probably in her early seventies. She had a thin, angular face. Her hair was greying and curly and she had a kind but sad face. She was going to have a serious operation and was very nervous about it. Prudence made a point of reassuring her and found the woman easy to talk to. She seemed to want to talk and told Prudence that she had had three children but was now a widow. One of her daughters had died with diphtheria when she was quite young which had been a great sorrow but she did still have one daughter who had a lovely little girl called Sarah. That seemed to be all that the woman wanted to tell her although Prudence was sure she had said she had had three children. She found herself liking this quiet, thoughtful patient, who said her name was Millie. It was obvious that s was worried about the operation but Prudence promised her that she would look after her when she came back to the ward and if she needed anything at all she would be there to care for all her needs.

Millie came through the operation without any problems and true to her word Prudence made sure that she was very well looked after when she returned to the ward.

She only had two visitors while she was in hospital. One of them was her daughter and the other a man whom the lady said was her boss from work. He was the man who owned 'The Strawberry' pub where she worked as a cleaner. He seemed a very nice man and was obviously very relieved that his lady friend was progressing well after her operation. Indeed, she was progressing so well that she was allowed to go home within ten days but not before asking Prudence to come and see her at her home in Douglas Terrace. The two ladies had become friends, and they were each benefiting from having someone to talk to and exchange confidences. Prudence became a regular visitor to Douglas Street and sometimes the man from 'The Strawberry' was there too. They were both so pleased that their friend Millie was getting so much better and Mr Riddell promised that if she continued to make this good progress he was going to take Prudence and Millie out for a meal, and perhaps a visit to the Tyne Theatre, on the West Road.

Before this happened, Prudence took her new friend out for short walks to build up her strength and one day they managed to walk as far as Leazes Park. It was springtime and the spring flowers were a lovely show of colour, which cheered them up immensely. They had both felt the chill of winter in their lives but it was now time to move on into the spring.

In the weeks that followed Millie gained strength and soon she was strong enough to walk with Prudence as far as 'The Strawberry', where Mr Riddell greeted them warmly. He was very happy to see his cleaner, or special friend as she now was, so well again. The nurse with her also looked much happier than when he had first met her, so it was good news all round.

Prudence was indeed looking and feeling so much happier. She had a very nice, more mature friend in Millie and a very nice young friend in Edith. Her confidence, which had taken a nasty knock when she and Samuel split up, was growing and her lovely new friends brought her a lot of happiness. She was never lonely. She still thought about Samuel and she would always love him and carry him in her heart, but she had forgiven him for breaking up with her, even though she would never understand why he did it. Never mind, she had moved on now and was actually dating someone else. It was none other than Dr Isaac. She had always liked him and had got to know him really well when she was helping the family after his wife died but she had never dreamt that one day she would be dating him. He was so kind and understanding and she knew that he missed his wife dreadfully, so she never thought of herself as taking on the role of his wife.

Prudence was not the only one going out with someone now. A very good friendship was developing between Millie and Jack Riddell. He had been surprised at his feelings for her when she was ill in hospital. He was very concerned that she was so ill and when she made such a good recovery he was so relieved. He felt very attracted to her and as they got to know one another better she had shared with him the story of her son's disappearance and the subsequent illness of her husband. It had been a very gruelling time nursing her husband and she had been extremely unhappy after her son left home and her husband had died. It had been a very dark time bringing back as it did the death of her oldest daughter. If it had not been for her youngest daughter Esther and her grandchild Sarah, she did not think she would have survived. Jack understood now how she had first appeared to him as a very unhappy person and he was glad that she was now much happier. He could not help hoping that one day her beloved son would get in touch with her again but he had to admit it seemed unlikely. He certainly looked to have been a very handsome young man, from the photograph on her mantlepiece.

As the weeks went by Millie and Jack drew closer and Jack, who was approaching 80 years old, decided he would ask Millie to marry him. She was only a year younger than him and if they were to have a life together the sooner they got married the better it would be. Millie was delighted when Jack proposed to her. She had grown to love him dearly and of course she accepted his proposal.They began to make plans immediately. The first people they told about their engagement were Isaac and Prudence who were delighted for their friends. Millie explained that they would only have a small wedding but she wanted it to be at St. Andrew's Church where her parents had married and where she had married Arthur over 50 years ago. Prudence would be her bridesmaid and Dr Isaac would walk her down the aisle.The wedding took place on a beautiful sunny day in June 1935 and Millie, who for so many years had felt she would never be truly happy again, had finally found that happiness.

Meanwhile what of Samuel? He was very, very miserable when he parted from Prudence. He missed her company so much and was again grateful for the friendship of Dr Isaac and Catherine, but when Catherine took ill, Samuel again felt that deep sense of loss because she had been such a good friend to him. Strangely enough after the tradgedy of Catherine's death, it became quite natural for Samuel, Isaac, and Prudence to meet up and help one another over their loss. Samuel was surprised how comfortable he was with the arrangement, as was Prudence. They went out walking and shared meals in their various homes, until Samuel who had always loved sport became very involved with the tennis club at the top of Osborne Road and he did not see his friends Isaac and Prudence quite so much. The Tennis Club was indoors which meant it was open throughout the year and he spent a lot of his time there. Isaac and Prudence continued to meet up socially and on one occasion when they were meeting up for a meal at her house Prudence asked Millie and Jack to join them. After that they all met up regularly and became very good friends, which was why they were the first people to know about Millie and Jack's engagement and they were very pleased to be involved in their wedding plans Millie and Jack often reminised about their wedding in the company of Isaac and Prudence.

Samuel still met up with Isaac and Prudence from time to time and he loved entertaining them in his Jesmond flat, but he had to say that his favourite visitors were Isaac and his family, Edith, Edward and Thomas. The children were all in their twenties now and had all sorts of interests but they all loved Samuel.They had spent so much time with him when they were younger and always enjoyed his company. When they all went out together it was usually to The Theatre Royal. It was a wonderful theatre which had begun its life on Mosley Street. It had opened on 21st January 1788 but it was demolished in 1836 by Mr Richard Grainger, a renowned architect of his time, who wanted to redevelop the centre of Newcastle. The theatre on Mosley Street was in the way of his development of Grey Street, but he was committed to rebuilding it and the new theatre opened in Grey Street in 1837 with a performance of Shakespeare's 'The Merchant of Venice'. The front of the theatre was specially designed with six huge Corinthian columns and looked magnificent.

From Isaac's family being very young, a visit to the theatre had always been an occasion and that sense of occasion had to be reflected in your mode of dress. Edith loved those occasions and usually designed herself a gown to wear. Her sewing machine was well used at such times. Her brothers still teased her about her appearance saying she was'over the top' but she never let it bother her too much.

# Chapter 24

It was on one of their Theatre visits that Samuel's life changed. Sometimes he felt his age and had resigned himself to being a bachelor for the rest of his life, but he really enjoyed the company of Isaacs's children and they helped him to have a younger outlook on life. He had never considered them as any more than friends but one evening when they all met up for a meal before the theatre, Edith arrived a little late. She always looked beautiful and as on other theatre occasions she wore a dress she had designed and made herself. On the evening in question, she looked almost ethereal in the dress she was wearing. It was made in a pale gold fabric and because she loved the Victorian syle of dress, it had a high frilled neckline, long tight sleeves with a frilled gold cuff, a tight waist, and a crinoline skirt. Around her shoulders she wore a gold threaded stole. Her beautiful fair hair was drawn back in a chignon, with some tendrils of it hanging down, to frame her pretty face.

She looked stunning and Samuel could hardly take his eyes off her all night. Suddenly he found himself wanting to be more than friends with Edith but then he had to consider that he was much older than her and she would never think of him in a romantic way. Samuel had never thought he would think romantically about another girl after Prudence and even now he dismissed his feelings. It was unthinkable that Edith would ever think of him as more than a friend.

Isaac was saying something about the fire which had occurred at the theatre in 1899, and which had gutted the building, but the interior was redesigned by Frank Matcham, the famous theatre architect and opened again in 1901. He heard Edith remark that she was very glad that the theatre had survived all its ill luck because it was her favourite place to be and he could not believe it when she leaned towards him and whispered 'especially if you are with me'. Samuel would have been very surprised to know that Edith actually thought he was wonderful. She always had since first knowing him. She had so enjoyed all the times she and her brothers had shared with him exploring Newcastle and all the long walks on the Town Moor and in the countryside, enjoying the fresh air and marvelling at the wonders of nature.

He had been so understanding when her beloved mother died and she had been in the depths of despair. He had listened endlessly to her tirades about how unfair life was and put up with her ill temper and tantrums, and inconsolable sobs and once when she told him that she was so angry she could punch somebody, he had said that she could punch him if it made her feel any better. Samuel was a tower of strength to her and had been her greatest comfort in the darkest days of her life. She loved him dearly and in the days and weeks ahead of that special theatre visit a deep and loving friendship developed between Samuel and Edith. All her friends envied her because Samuel was so good looking and such a gentleman. Samuel had been worried that Isaac would think he was too old for his daughter but Isaac could see how happy Samuel made his daughter and he was delighted when Samuel and Edith announced their engagement.

Isaac of course was a much happier man himself at that time because he realised that Prudence was coming to mean a great deal to him. He had loved his wife Catherine deeply and still missed her terribly but his life was becoming meaningful again. He had always admired the dedication Prudence showed in her nursing and he could not thank her enough for the love and compassion she had shown his family after Catherine's death.She had such a loving nature and had quietly got on caring for them all in a most unassuming way. She had never been an intrusion and he knew Catherine would have been so grateful for her care and attention to her family. He came to realise that he loved her very much and so, not long after Edith announced her engagement, her father had his own engagement to announce. His three children totally approved because they had come to regard Prudence as a mother figure in their lives.

With two weddings to organise, Isaac's family was very busy. Samuel's wedding was to be held in St. George's Church in Jesmond, very near to their family home. All three of Isaac's children had been baptised there, and attended the church at special times of the year, namely Christmas and Easter. Catherine's funeral had been held there and Edith was absolutely happy to be married there because somehow she would feel her mother was close to her. She also knew that her mother would have been very happy that she was getting married to Samuel. He was a great friend of hers.

St George's Church was built at the top of Osborne Road and was built in 1888 because the population was growing rapidly in Jesmond and a Parish Church was needed. Charles Mitchell was a wealthy local resident, living in Jesmond Towers near Jesmond Dene and he had offered to pay for a completely new church and vicarage to be built on part of his estate. He bought a temporary iron church which had been used in St. George's, Cullercoats but it became too small for the growing congregation. He said he would pay for a grander church on the condition that he could have the church designed to his liking. The foundation stone was laid in in January 1887 and a young architect was appointed to prepare plans. Charles Mitchell was heard to comment, 'it is not what it costs but what is best' and so the very best materials were used. The church was consecrated on October the 16th 1888. It could hold 700 people and had cost £30,000 to build.

There was great excitement in preparing for the wedding. Edith, as expected, designed and made her own wedding dress. It was a beautiful guipure lace coat with crystal buttons down the front and a train at the back edged with the crystal buttons. The coat covered a crystal organza gown trimmed at the neck with crystals. A long lace veil cascaded down the back of the dress to meet the train and the whole effect was absolutely stunning. Even her brothers for once did not criticise her style of dress. They were so proud of their beautiful sister and Edith in turn was very proud of her handsome groomsmen. They had made a great effort to look their very best in their wedding attire. She had thought they might grumble about having to dress up in their wedding suits because they liked to be dressed more casually but there were no complaints. She heaved a sigh of relief. Samuel looked amazing too in his wedding clothes. It was the happiest day of his life. It was a pity that Millie and Jack, the friends of Isaac and Prudence, could not be present. Jack had hurt his back when lifting a very heavy crate at 'The Strawberry' and Millie did not want to leave him alone while he was in such pain. She wanted him to be fit enough to attend Isaac's wedding in two months' time.

Fortunately they were able to attend the wedding at St. Phillip's Church in the west of the city not far from Snow Street School which Jack and Millie had attended all those years ago. The vicar of the church knew Prudence, who had attended his church quite frequently at one time. He was very pleased to be marrying her in his church.

Jack and Millie were very early when they took up their seats in St Phillip's Church. The Groom and his best man had not yet arrived. When they came to sit down at the front of the church Milie could not help noticing that the dark curly hair of the best man, curled into the nape of his neck just as her son Samuel's used to do. In fact he looked to be the same build as her son, tall, dark and slim as he had been. Funny that she was thinking so much about Samuel and when the best man moved out to give the rings to the vicar she saw his face. She knew that face. There was not another like it. She had dreamt of seeing that face again for so long that she could not believe it, but her eyes did not deceive her. It was indeed her beloved son Samuel. She thought she was going to faint and had to quickly take her husband's arm, which caused Jack to look at Millie. He was concerned to see her ashen face and to note that she was trembling. Something was the matter but she managed to give him a reassuring smile and he kept his arm around her for the remainder of the service...

Somehow Millie contained herself until the end of the service and until they had left the church but she could hardly wait to make herself known to her son. At the first opportunity, in a moment of pure joy, Millie wrapped her arms around Samuel and clung to him as if she would never let him go. After his initial bewilderment and some sort of explanation from this lady, Samuel was overjoyed to meet his mother from whom he had been separated so long. He had never thought he would see his mother again and to know that she was alive and well and could be part of his life again was wonderful.

The weeks and months ahead passed in a blur because there was so much to find out and talk about. There were so many reunions and so many tears of joy and happiness. Millie was estatic with joy to have her son back again and Samuel could not believe that he now had his own family again. Esther was delighted to be reunited with her brother and he loved his new found niece who told him that she had done so much wishing that he would come home one day. In fact she was sure now that there was a fairy godmother because her wish had been granted.

In all the talking that was done in the weeks following the wedding one thing was never talked about and that was of course the accident at the Rowing Regatta all those years ago. Samuel never spoke about it because he was determined that no-one would ever know the truth about his father. His resolve to keep that secret to the end of his life never wavered.

Several months later there was even more joy for Samuel and Millie. Edith gave birth to a son. Samuel was a father himself now and the feeling of pride that he felt as he held his son in his arms for the first time was overwhelming. He was sure of one thing and that was that he would never ever betray his son.

The memory of his own father's betrayal would never be forgotten but it was buried at the bottom of his heart. It had been wonderful getting to know his mother again and he was as determined as ever that his mother would never know the truth about his father.

He would make sure that his son would have a good education, as he had had at Snow Street school and then Armstrong College.

He would make his son proud of him. He would try to give his son as much knowledge as his father had given to him and one day he would take his son down to the River Tyne and stop on one of the bridges which his father had told him so much about. He would make sure that his son worked hard so that he would get a good job and perhaps be an engineer like him. He would tell him about all the famous men and especially the engineers who had made Newcastle great. He pictured himself playing football with his son, who was called Arthur after his grandfather. Edith had insisted on giving him that name in memory of his father, though if she had known the truth about him, Samuel was sure she would not have given him the name Arthur. His middle name was Samuel, which again was Edith's choice, and he certainly was very pleased about that. Millie of course was delighted with the choice of names. Arthur and Samuel were the two heroes of her life. She lived until she was 90 years of age and never stopped thanking God that he had allowed Samuel back into her life and she saw as much of her son and grandson as she could until the end of her life.

Prudence had a very happy marriage to Isaac and whenever she met Samuel, which was often, because he and Isaac were still good friends, she could speak to him without the slightest hint of regret because she loved her husband Isaac very much indeed. She and Samuel remained good friends to the end of their lives.

Edith and Samuel had a very happy marriage and when their son and daughter started school Edith went back to college and gained a degree in art and design. Their daughter, born two years after her brother, was called Molly. Samuel had insisted on that name though why that particular name Edith never discovered. She would have been happier calling her Catherine after her own mother but she accepted Samuel's choice. They decided on two more names for Molly. She was to be Molly Catherine Rachel in memory of two special people, Edith's mother and Samuel's sister. Both parents were content with that.

Samuel was promoted at Parsons a number of times because he had proved himself to be a very good engineer. (His father would have been very pleased and proud.) He could afford now to buy an expensive house in a good area and he and Edith and the children moved house to live in Gosforth, a prestigious area of Newcastle, north of the city. He often thought about William Armstrong and his generosity in the way he used his wealth to help his employees and support charities, and he and Edith gave generously to many charities now that they had the means to do so.

Samuel was so glad that in the end he had returned to Newcastle. He had gained so much by doing so and realised he should not have stayed away for so long. Newcastle was in his eyes the best town in the whole country and there was no other place he would rather be.

**THE END**

Lightning Source UK Ltd.
Milton Keynes UK
UKHW01f0000180518
322737UK00001B/27/P